Black, White, and **RED** All Over

A Gritty, Current,
Clean Christian Mystery

Deeann D. Mathews

Table of Contents

Acknowledgments

This book represents a journey in writing that was unusual. There are a number of people to thank along the way, only a few of whom I knew before March 2019, while at the time of this writing, it is only October 2019!

First of all, thank You to the God and Father of my Lord and Savior Jesus Christ and my family, all of whom encouraged me to keep writing after major injury sidetracked my entire life for a year. The Lord Himself led me to a new writing platform on a blockchain while I was actually researching a musician I wanted to write music for. I had been praying for a way into understanding and mining cryptocurrency for some time before that, and the Lord granted me my request in two ways!

Second, thank you to my many friends and encouragers on the best version of that new writing platform – Hive (https://hive.blog OR https://peakd.com), which allows writers to earn Hive, a cryptocurrency, for their writing on the platform. That's not a bad incentive, but that's not the main thing for me. I owe a special thanks to Ms. Marianne West and the folks in the Freewrite House community. One of their writing prompts for their daily freewrite caused me to pull out a detective character I created in my twenties – Ironwood Hamilton – and the rest of this is mystery history in the making! *Black, White, and RED All Over* began as a long serial story that I published for Freewrite House. The story came to attention and acclaim there, and will forever be on the Hive blockchain in its original format. Hive has a great audience for writers, especially in the freewriting community. Without the support of the Freewrite House and the community around it, this book never could have happened, so a special thanks to my fellow writers there!

Third, thank you to the naysayer user on the old version of the platform who told me, "You can't make a living on this"! Without that challenge, it is very likely that I would not have pushed so hard in creating extra content to find the limits of what could be done, and thus have pushed myself through limits on how much I can write and publish in a short period of time that is good writing!

Lastly, you, the reader, will get to judge how good this is for yourself, so, last but certainly not least, thank you for reading, and if you would return to Amazon to drop an honest review, I would deeply appreciate it!

Chapter 1: The New Newspaper

"It used to be 'what's that black and white and read all over?' was a joke told about the newspaper, but every newspaper in the hands of racist reactionaries in the South has indeed been red all over – soaked with the blood of innocent Black people brutalized and slaughtered over lies in print that continue to this day.

"No more will we allow the wholesale placarding of racist tomes about ourselves and our children to pass for news. No more will we not have a voice to raise in challenge. No more shall we, the Black populations of Tinyville, Littleburg, Miniopolis, Smallwood, Shortport, Big Loft, and the rural countryside be passively painted as savages while the real savages sit comfortably in places of law, commerce, and politics. Be it known to all Virginia: those days are over! Hereby understand that the *Lofton County Free Voice* will roar back at the voices of racist reactionary news, beginning in Tinyville, then across Lofton County, then to the uttermost parts of Virginia!"

Captain Ironwood Hamilton and Lieutenant Patrick O'Reilly of Tinyville's two-man police force stood at the nearest public bulletin board nearest the police station, reading what they had been reading, over and over again, on their regular dawn walk through the town.

The lieutenant was 25 years old, medium height and build, with bright red hair, ruddy skin, green eyes, and a shocking Southern drawl (unless you know the Scotch-Irish history of the southeastern United States).

The captain was 45 years old, six feet tall, sinewy, with iron-gray eyes and hair to match. His features looked like something that those Southern artists who loved to carve Confederates out of marble would have adored – classic, strong features, handsome, calm, and resolute. The slight pinch in those features from the sudden headache the captain was experiencing would of course have been glossed over.

"Wow," said Lieutenant O'Reilly. "Have ever you read such bombast in all your life, Captain?"

Captain Ironwood Hamilton shook his head slowly, slowly because of the headache that was increasing every second.

"It's only bombast if the *Lofton County Free Voice* can't do what it says. I rather think it can, or at least can make a gallant effort."

Lieutenant O'Reilly's green eyes got wide.

"Captain, you're not serious! A Black newspaper? In Lofton County? They won't last a week!"

7

Captain Hamilton shook his head again, and restrained his urge to rub his throbbing temples.

"It's not 1819, and these are not amateurs we are dealing with. Just from this first issue, I know they have a good chunk of money in hand, dedicated people, and good strategic and tactical sense."

"How?"

"Look at the quality of the paper and ink – excellent for something the editors of the *Free Voice* have to know is going to be exposed to the elements and the anger of a good portion of 72 percent of the town. It's a 20 weight 11X17 paper, with first-class laser ink on a new printer."

"How do you know it's new?"

"Printed items, particularly in color, have less sharply defined edges the older the printer gets – there's a bit less precision. Anyhow: one has to consider this being $4 per sheet – a little less with discounts on bulk printing, but assuming just Tinyville for the moment, there are at least 100 of these if the town is saturated like we have seen on the streets we have checked. That's $400 in printing costs alone. None of that was spent here – either in Roanoke or Big Loft, where they have the kind of print shops that can do this kind of work.

"Which brings me to the other point: this issue is composed of six different articles, written by various people on various kinds of computers and word processors, but all of whom have the same desktop publishing software. Look here at the different articles. You can see the mild glitching in spacing between lines and within lines of text in the articles, although the frames that the stories go into remain perfect.

"Someone sent out the template with the editorial in place. The first person to receive it flowed his contribution into the space designed for it, saved it, and sent to the next writer who likewise flowed her contribution in. The last person who got his or her article in sent it to whoever was going to give it a final look before it went out.

"The point, Lieutenant: the paper is decentralized, and the writers beside the editor himself have used pen names of great figures in Black history. They know better than to present an easy target. As it stands, our local domestic terrorists would have to burn down the print shops in Big Loft and Roanoke to stop this paper from coming out."

"They're not spoiling for that big a fight," Lieutenant O'Reilly said.

"No. But the *Lofton County Free Voice* is trying to provoke a reaction, and they'll get it. The *Tinyville Times* and the papers of the other mentioned towns will lash back, say too much, and thus help the *Free Voice* put pressure on toward its true object – ."

9

In the distance, the captain and the lieutenant heard the phones in the police station began to ring. It was 6:30am, and Tinyville was beginning to wake up. Like Captain Hamilton's headache, the volume of calls would continue to increase through the morning. Indeed, Tinyville and the whole of Lofton County were seeing red all over, everywhere the provocative new paper was posted.

Not that the two-man police force in Tinyville took all those calls. The non-emergency voice message service picked up all the calls, transcribed them, and printed them for quick review – either the lieutenant or the captain scanned them periodically for police matters, but left the complaints to accumulate. Woe be to the citizen who called through 9-11 about the paper! Captain Hamilton answered those in such a way that the offending person would *never* make that abuse of emergency services again.

Meanwhile, the morning went on. Captain Hamilton handled five interviews for three open lieutenant positions that morning, and then returned that afternoon to the task that had cost the Tinyville force those three lieutenants. The captain had the grim task of going through the 68 percent of cases handled by the department in the decade before he came that showed clear racial bias in treatment and investigation of Tinyville's

Black population.

There was sufficient reason for the thundering indignation of the *Lofton County Free Voice*. Some of those cases had led to wrongful convictions, and the captain was painstakingly sorting those out and slating them to be re-opened. In 10 years, there was a goodly bunch, and therefore a goodly bunch of innocent men and women incarcerated for crimes that they didn't commit – or never even happened. Some cases had been made up out of thin air!

The problem for Captain Hamilton was two-fold: he knew that if 68 percent of cases had clearly gone wrong, then there was no trusting *anything* the department had done in the last ten years when it came to Black people. *Every* conviction obtained on the county and state level of a Black person that came out of Tinyville was suspect.

The other problem: while working through that much legal mess was a process best done carefully, and therefore had to be done slowly with only one man having access to the material, 28 percent of Tinyville was tired of waiting for the truth to be brought out. The paper's launch was provocative. The Freedom of Information Act request it had made of the Tinyville police department would be downright explosive, no matter how Captain Hamilton handled it.

In the afternoon, citizens of Tinyville incensed by the *Lofton County Free Voice's* intrusive launch began coming to the police station to see why their complaint calls were not being answered. They were stunned to see their rather excited statements presented to them in writing, and then to hear the grim gravity of Captain Hamilton's voice as he said, over and over and over again, "Although I understand your concern, we do not have departmental resources to spare to respond to and investigate non-criminal matters."

Lieutenant O'Reilly marveled at how many people seemed to *want it to be a crime* that the descendants of the enslaved could make use of the rights of American citizens in public expression, just like everyone else in Virginia. They rhetorically danced around it, but, it was at the heart of the dance.

Captain Hamilton sat like a block of marble in his department's heather-gray uniform, and held his ground. Out of the corner of his eye, he could see through the window screen a set of mahogany-colored fingers, holding a notebook that was bobbing up and down – being written in.

All the carrying on of many White citizens of Tinyville about the launch of the *Lofton County Free Voic*e at the police department – all their wanting the police to do what it had traditionally done since the end of the Civil War in assisting in the snatching of hard-won freedoms away from Black people – was being recorded and would be reported. There was a long line urging that, including prominent town figures. The embarrassment was going to be severe. Captain Hamilton's concern was that the police department itself not get caught up in any way. The Freedom of Information Act request sitting in the captain's desk would be more than trouble enough.

Not only that. Lieutenant O'Reilly had kept track of social media, and had found something interesting. Instead of the new paper having a website that could be attacked, what people were doing was taking pictures of the first edition of the *Lofton County Free Voice* and its articles, and then putting them on their own social media. Further decentralization, since now to shut down the spread of the news, a whole bunch – dozens, becoming hundreds, becoming thousands – of social media accounts would all have to be shut down.

The local crowd most interested in that shutdown likely did not have the kind of sophistication to catch up – and besides, the diversity of the social media was too much to cope with, given that Black Junction and Blaggenuf and Hive and Palnet and Dtube and Threespeak were not likely to bow to the pressures to class the new paper as "hate speech" that the big social media giants might come under. *The Lofton County Free Voice*, and its six articles, were spreading far and wide quickly, and also into corners where it could not be easily stifled, from whence its message could be summoned to confront its ideological foes at the touch of a button.

Near the close of the day, Captain Hamilton looked at the information Lieutenant O'Reilly was compiling, and pondered the magnitude of what they both were seeing.

"I see what you were saying earlier, Captain," Lieutenant O'Reilly said. "That may not be bombast after all, the stuff that little editorial was talking … they are making quite a go at it, already! Oh … look here, Captain. The paper and all its articles have now passed the 10,000th mark for shares, and there must be a million likes and thousands upon thousands of interesting comments … ."

"We ain't seen nothing yet," the captain said. "Lofton County is not prepared for its Black population to talk back with *equal strength of voice,* but it had better get prepared, and so had we. In that stack of non-emergency calls are the calls of our fellow police officers in Big Loft, Littleburg, Miniopolis, Smallwood, Shortport, and the county itself.

Their day has been much like ours. I think an impromptu working dinner

may be in order."

Chapter 2: A Difficult Dinner

Although Captain Hamilton was a tea-totaler, he had a favorite bar – the Midway Bar and Grill, the last stop after Big Loft before hitting Miniopolis and the rest of Lofton County's truly small towns and rural countryside. Midway had fabulous barbecue, and was a favorite spot for the region's veteran population as well as lovers of barbecue all over southern Virginia. Ironwood Hamilton was both Major Hamilton, U.S. Army Reserve, and also a grillmaster with little time on his hands.

While he waited on his fellow officers, the captain ordered a huge to-go order for his wife and children – three kinds of links, short ribs, burnt ends, chicken, and his wife's favorite, tri-tip – to enjoy that night and for his wife to get set up for the weekend.

"You must spend half your check in here on barbecue," the waitress who served him said, with a smile.

"My wife says that with the exception of what I grill myself, this is her favorite barbecue in all of Virginia," he said, "and since I don't have time to barbecue right now, this is the least I can do to keep her happy."

The cook, Rufus Johnson, came out of the back at the sound of the captain's voice, his ebony skin glowing from the heat of the massive grill in the back, and his smile glowing with joy.

"Dropping your check with us again?"

"Well, if a man has to burn through his money, the best place to do it would be on your grill, Mr. Johnson."

Mr. Johnson's laughter boomed all the way through the bar, a deep, rattling bass that startled a few of the captain's guests as they came through to the grill side of Midway.

Lieutenant O'Reilly had only been part of Tinyville's police force two weeks longer than Captain Hamilton, who himself had only been in office for three months. The lieutenant had been snatched up right out of police academy because of the emergency that had caused Tinyville to ask Major Hamilton to also come home: Captain Sidney had a heart attack behind the wheel and gone off the road, killing his favorite lieutenant as well. That had brought Tinyville's police force down to three. Lieutenant O'Reilly had scarcely gotten through orientation, such as it was, before Captain Hamilton had arrived and essentially blown up the whole process by firing the entire old guard.

Thus, Lieutenant O'Reilly and Captain Hamilton were still getting to know each other, and the lieutenant was constantly surprised by the mature man's way of approaching law enforcement and life. He was also surprised by the effect the captain had on the people around him. It didn't take a great detective to look at some of the older police officers and realize they drank pretty heavily in their off time. Occupational hazard: being a police officer was not a stress-free life, even in rural Virginia. Still, not one guest ordered more than one beer in the presence of their host. None of them even over-ate.

Something about Captain Hamilton, calmly and genially eating his Caesar's Grill Salad with no dressing and a glass of sparking tonic water with no gin added on the side, just caused every man at the table to find his discipline. Lieutenant O'Reilly had seen a Black man do that before – since Thomas Stepforth Sr. had come to town, everything and everyone around him had just gotten in order. None of his grandchildren, his nieces and nephews, and none of their friends had been anywhere near legitimate police action since. Yet the lieutenant had not gotten to see how a mature family leader could have that effect on people up close, not until he sat down at the right hand of his commander.

Dinner before the business was relaxed. Despite the higher discipline at the table, most of the officers still seemed very much at home with each other. Most of them were Captain Hamilton's age or older; the oldest, the hawk-like, white-haired Captain Angler from Smallwood, was at least 65. Lieutenant O'Reilly was the youngest, and drank in the stories of the experienced officers with amazement.

It was not long before the lieutenant could sense why Captain Hamilton had fired the old guard, and why the Black population of Lofton County was fed up. It was not the racial slurs that slipped out of his fellow officers' mouths – at least at first, they were too professional for all that in public. Yet nowhere in the thinking of most of them did Black people exist as more than a hassle, an inconvenience, a problem – at best. Some of the comments about the *Lofton County Free Voice* indicated the old suspicions and hatred were neither dead nor sleeping, 154 years after the end of chattel slavery.

Captain Hamilton let his guests get their day off their chest, and then ordered dessert: a huge pound cake, warm and fresh from the oven. While that was being gratefully eaten, he commenced the business.

"So, like I said when I called, we're here to figure out what to do with the coming of the *Lofton County Free Voice* – I expect that all of you were inundated with calls."

They had been. Littleburg's police switchboard had crashed, complete with arcs and sparks and a small fire. In Miniopolis, the officer

19

assigned to the switchboard had saved it by simply turning it off every thirty minutes and letting it cool down, leading to a flood of angry callers coming to the office, every thirty minutes. In Shortport, citizens had skipped the non-emergency line entirely and overloaded 9-11, which had caused a car crash to not get reported in a timely fashion. That call had to bounce all the way to Big Loft, which had big-city switchboards that could handle the flood of calls, before any EMTs could be sent to the crash.

"And you know there is going to be trouble behind that," Captain Angler said. "One of those new-money Slocum brats, in his Lamborghini, upset with us because we couldn't get someone out to unbend his fender and change his tire in two minutes flat."

(Translation: a "new-money" Slocum was one whose family branch had got their money after the Civil War, whereas the old-money Slocums were extinct – or at least, the old money had been extinct since 1870).

"Well, look, Angler," said Lieutenant Grattan from Shortport, "it was a sort of an emergency. His girlfriend's mascara and half her hair color might have melted and run in a few minutes more of all that heat!"

On the stories went until they were finished, and then Captain Hamilton shared how he and Lieutenant O'Reilly had gotten an update for their phone service, and Tinyville's switchboard had survived. This changed the mood at the table entirely; relief and smiles broke out, for a little while. But..."

"Now all we have to do is figure out what we are going to do about the paper!" an officer said.

"Oh, yes," sad Captain Hamilton, "which is why I called us together."

Lieutenant O'Reilly nearly jumped at the eagerness – nay, almost soul hunger – of most of the officers at that table at the thought of the brilliant Captain Hamilton devising a strategy to deal with the paper and the Black people behind it, in the "good ol' boys" style. With the exception of one grim and quiet officer of about Captain Hamilton's age with a strikingly familiar appearance, the rest leaned forward, hungrily, as if someone had offered them a nice, juicy, *black* burnt end …

"Have y'all decided what to do with those Freedom of Information Act requests yet?"

The shock, the disgust, the disappointment – all of it was equally palpable as the officers jumped back. Some of them looked stung, as though Captain Hamilton had slapped them in the face. One of them, his face red, spat out – "What do you mean, have y'all decided – I ripped the one that came to my office up and put it in the round file *and* burned it! Who do these news Negroes think they are, demanding our files – Obama ain't in office no more!"

The table froze up at first, but, broad agreement spread over many of the faces as the seconds passed.

"I am inclined to agree in substance with Captain Bragg," said Captain Johnston of Shortport's police force. "Although the requests are indeed backed by federal law, there is likely not going to be serious enforcement of that law from the present administration. There is no need for these people, who have no knowledge of the working of law, its enforcement, and investigative techniques to have all that information they cannot possibly rightly interpret in hand, to bandy about to the press and social media and other sources of needless agitation."

Captain Angler was more circumspect.

"My son was kind enough to get on the computer and look a bunch of stuff up for me about this thing when I got my request letter. His research says that there are only nine legitimate reasons to refuse a Freedom of Information Act request. One of them would be active investigations that can be compromised, but unless we reopen ten years of cases, we don't have a legal leg to stand on in order to refuse."

"Angler – I would expect that you of all people –."

"I'm 68 years old, Johnston. I lived through the civil rights period. The longer the thing stretches out in the press, the worse all of us and Lofton County are going to look. We answer the requests, and we thus show we have nothing to be ashamed of. We bury them in the data they want. They've got papers to get out; the storm of old news will fade out as new things happen, long before they get through all of that.

"If we dig in, even if the local courts decide in our favor, that paper will take all that time and agitate, agitate, agitate. Those who feel they have been mistreated will air their stories to fill the gap, and any attempt on our part to answer the mis-characterizations will be met with, 'Well, just release the records and we'll decide for ourselves.' By the time we have to give up the records, the damage will be done. Law men who have done absolutely nothing wrong will not be safe in Virginia, the anger will be so high – and then they will camp on every detail they find suspicious, week after week after week. Ten years of information – they won't be done for at least two, tarring and feathering all of us in public, and getting that rag read seriously across the country and the world."

Lieutenant O'Reilly looked at Captain Hamilton, aghast – but there was nothing reassuring in that grim marble front, yet.

"Not only that, gentlemen – there's that pesky Innocence Project, holed up as close as the University of Virginia at Charlottesville," said Lieutenant Hill of Littleburg. "You would think the boys could have at least stopped by there if they had wanted to do something helpful before that little girl was sadly killed –."

"Ms. Heather Heyer, 32 years old," Captain Hamilton interjected softly, "killed by one in that lawless mob."

"Yes, that girl," said Lieutenant Hill. "Anyway, imagine the situation if we draw this thing out and they end up getting the information later and calling on the Innocence Project to look into it. Once that happens, if there are any innocent n*****s we have inadvertently helped to put back to work for Virginia, and those folks find them, the scandal will go on for years. It will outlast *all* of our careers, except our new boy, O'Reilly here."

The new boy's head was spinning. Only the steady presence of Captain Hamilton was holding him steady.

"Come on – I can't believe you all are talking like this!" Captain Bragg cried. "This state has gone through a lot in the last 158 years not to have to go through this with these people!"

A deep sigh from the only officer quieter than Captain Hamilton at the table, his dark eyes emanating the sorrow that framed his grim face as thickly as his white-flecked black hair– and suddenly, Lieutenant O'Reilly realized why his face was *so* familiar in Virginia ...

"Now, don't you start, Lee!" Captain Bragg snapped. "Just because my great-great-grandfather messed up a few times and because your great-great-great-uncle had to sign the whole thing off in 1865 doesn't mean I need a history lesson from you! I already know what happened!"

Captain Henry Fitzhugh Lee of Big Loft's police force leaned forward in his chair and gave Captain Bragg a glare so cold that one would have thought it was around February of 1865. Like his cousin Captain Hamilton, Captain Lee was new in Big Loft's police force, and like Captain Hamilton, he knew he had a mess on his hands, very little time to solve it, and no patience for bombast from anyone. His tone was quiet, but as withering as a freezing cold day.

"Captain Bragg," he said, "we've known each other since childhood, so you ought to know by now that I wouldn't even waste my time on you like that at a time like this."

Captain Bragg looked as if he had been slapped again.

"What I was about to say," the captain said, "is that we in Big Loft have a Freedom of Information Act office that has determined what you have found out, Captain Angler. The decision is up to the police commissioner, and comes down to whether it is determined that some cases need to be reopened."

"About how many would it take to stop a Freedom of Information Act request like this?" said Captain Johnston.

Captain Lee sighed again.

"That's not even the right question, but –."

"Look here, Lee, we know your family fell from Olympus, but still –."

"*Stop that,*" Captain Lee snapped. "There is no time for that foolishness!"

Captain Lee's orders were instantly obeyed; silence resumed at table.

"Have any of y'all *yet* all been through the files these people are asking for?"

"I have," Captain Hamilton said.

Silence around the rest of the table.

"Fine," Captain Lee said. "The rest of you haven't been through them because you lived what is there, or you just don't remember and just don't care – but you're asking questions like we just need to find some simple trick or loophole out of this mess. *There is none.* Y'all just want to know if somehow there is a magic number of cases we have to halfheartedly reopen in order to stall this request. *There isn't."*

"Are you sure?" Lieutenant Wells said.

Captain Lee sighed again.

"Suppose we were to try to find that proverbial back door – Southern white men in Virginia, heirs of the Founders, reduced to desperately trying to slink through a back door – pick a number! Any number! What do you think, gentlemen? That Freedom of Information Act request encompasses all 80 miles of Lofton County – the sheriff's office, the five towns, and Big Loft – for the last ten years. How many cases do you think we would have to reopen in total to stop a Freedom of Information Act request that big?"

After a few moments, Lieutenant Pemberton sighed.

"I get it," he said. "Pretty darn near all of them."

"What would your ideal number be, Pemberton – you've got half the problem solved, but let's keep going."

"200 cases, county wide."

"That's a nice, conservative estimation," Captain Lee said. "Anyone else?"

"One tenth of that," Captain Bragg spat. "This defeatism makes me sick."

The veins in Captain Lee's neck began to stand out; he was very, very angry, but maintained the cold tone in his voice.

"Be patient, Captain Bragg. In a few moments, you'll learn the difference between defeatism and defeat – anyone else?"

Captain Angler had caught the wind of where this was going; his face collapsed in a colossal frown.

"500 cases – 50 for each year," he said.

"With age and experience, at last we begin to hear a little common sense," Captain Lee said. "Assume that was the number – that would lead to scandal enough."

"I tell you, you make me sick, Lee!" Captain Bragg spat.

"Not as sick as I am about to make you," Captain Lee said. "If the numbers hold in your office, and all the rest of your offices, like they hold in mine, *every case involving an African American in Lofton County in the last ten years needs to be re-examined, and as many as 80 percent of the convictions may need to be overturned – and the world is about to know it!"*

Forks were dropped. Beverages were knocked over. Pound cake

was choked on, and Heimlich maneuvers had to be applied, spreading cake crumbs and half-chewed cake across the table.

"Well, I had just about lost my appetite anyway," Captain Angler said.

Anger gave way to sorrow again in Captain Lee's face.

"You are blessed, Captain Angler. You can retire out of this mess. I'd start drawing down that 401K as fast as I could, starting Monday. The rest of us – 20 years or more from retirement age. You're blessed, Lieutenant O'Reilly, to be very young, and fresh, and green. You can still go do something else, easily. And, Captain Hamilton, you're blessed because you are new, and at least made the right first steps *before* that Freedom of Information Act request came. If you don't survive in Tinyville, the Army will gladly have you back, full-time. Me? I already know I'm going back to the Army, or I will retire with 23 years of service. The rest of you? Plus-40 and with 10 and more years creating what is in those files?"

Captain Lee was kind enough not to say the rest. Captain Bragg thus flared up again.

"Well, I don't regret any of it – these people have to be kept under control or you see what they do! This is your fault anyway, Captain

Hamilton!"

"Oh?" Captain Hamilton said, with a disarming smile. "What did I do?"

"You handled that whole mess at the high school without the firmness necessary, and gave these people an opening to think they could get away with this kind of stuff!"

"The Freedom of Information Act request is dated two weeks before that happened," Captain Hamilton said evenly.

Captain Bragg sputtered and coughed. Lieutenant O'Reilly desperately hoped his attempt to stifle his laughter was not visible to the rest. However, Captain Lee saw it; his dark eyes lightened up, just a little.

"Besides that, Captain Bragg, no crime had been committed. Once you have done real violence, if you have a functioning conscience at all, you seek not to do it again unless it is absolutely necessary. I know that not everyone, owing to lack of experience or lack of conscience, can understand that, but –."

Captain Bragg turned the color of a tomato, while the grim features of Captain Lee brightened all the way up.

"-- It is what it is, Captain Bragg," Captain Hamilton finished, and then picked up his glass of tonic water and drank the last of it.

Captain Bragg had nothing else to say for the moment, and neither did Captain Lee, but the latter seemed much more satisfied than the former.

"Well," said Lieutenant Hill, "it looks like we have two options. The Angler Option: respond to the Freedom of Information Act request with excruciating detail and hope some other news comes along to drown it out, or, the Bragg Option: make them fight it out in the courts, and hope for the best. Deputy Alexander, what do you think Sheriff Nottingham's position is going to be?"

"We're in the same position as Captain Lee in Big Loft," Deputy Alexander said. "Our legal people are saying we either reopen the cases and thus get a legitimate reason, or we have to comply with the Freedom of Information Act request. The problem for those of you that want to hold out is going to be that if county and Big Loft go, and Smallwood goes as well, there's no chance in that much data that they aren't going to find something – the pressure on the rest of you will become immense, as will the pressure on the courts to force the rest out."

"Which is why we *all* have to hold out!" Captain Bragg said through clenched teeth.

"But Captain Bragg," said Deputy Alexander, "you're not listening. It's not in my hands. It's not in Captain Lee's hands either. We don't get to make those decisions."

"Well, who do I need to speak to?" Captain Bragg said. "I was listening – if we don't take our chances *we don't have a chance!*"

"Call the office Monday, and I'll put you through to Sheriff Nottingham," said Deputy Alexander.

Captain Lee drew out his pen and wrote on a clean napkin – "Here is the number of the police commissioner's office in Big Loft – Commissioner Orton Thomas."

"I'm surprised I didn't have to shame it out of you, Lee."

"I was sparing you the trouble of coming into the 21st century with your ideas, and having to use Google."

Captain Hamilton intervened by saying something, but poor Lieutenant O'Reilly coughed and sneezed and wheezed so hard that he didn't hear it.

"And on that note," Captain Hamilton said after he thumped his young lieutenant on the back like it was really necessary, "let's adjourn. I think we know where we are now."

"We don't know where you are," Lieutenant Hill said.

"That's because I don't know yet," Captain Hamilton said. "I will let all of you know, when I have made my decision."

No sooner were they outside and a little way from the rest did Lieutenant O'Reilly turn to his commander.

"Is it really that bad, sir?"

"It is, Lieutenant," the captain said grimly. "Notice how most of our colleagues talked about it. No thought as to what they have done in terms of the actual people they have done it to. Just cases, and how do we all escape the consequences that are coming. It is that bad, Lieutenant."

"What are we going to do?"

"I don't know yet. I know there is another way beyond what Captain Bragg and Captain Angler are proposing, and I know that unlike Captain Lee and Deputy Alexander, the buck stops on me. I also know Who knows."

"Who knows?"

Captain Hamilton pointed upward with a smile.

"He does!"

"Oh, of course!"

"Aren't you glad you don't have to depend on me and I don't have to depend on me either?" Captain Hamilton said with a smile. "We'll get home and get into prayer and then into bed, and we know the Lord will show us what way to go."

"How much time do we have left?"

"Just eight days, Lieutenant. Just enough time to prepare a data dump if we wanted to do that – but Deputy Alexander is right: it wouldn't work even if we tried it. Captain Angler is not up for that kind of fight. He may retire and leave a lieutenant to do the dump, but he is not going to go through all that. He knows there is no point. Every tree in the wood south of Smallwood surely knows why there is no point in Captain Angler and his crew fighting."

Lieutenant O'Reilly shuddered.

"You mean –."

"Yes, strange fruit," Captain Hamilton said, "and plenty of it. Maybe not in the last ten years, but still, once that floodgate of the last ten years opens up, that will be enough. The stories will all start coming out, for the past fifty. Captain Angler has been in that office for fifty years. He thinks, because he has forgotten things as we all do over time, that there's enough good policing in the last ten years so that the *Lofton County Free Voice* will get bogged down and then distracted away."

"Captain Bragg will be up first thing on Monday, trying to convince county and the commissioner in Big Loft that there is no way forward but to fight. If you think Captain Lee was giving him a hard time –."

Lieutenant O'Reilly broke out laughing at last.

"It was like watching a loud toy poodle barking at a pit bull – two pit bulls when he came after you!"

"Captain Bragg doesn't know how he is," Captain Hamilton said. "He and his crew have made a career making themselves feel big by bullying people who can't afford to lash back – until now. He still won't get it after tomorrow, either."

"I'm surprised Captain Lee didn't get the message over to him that it ain't about to work!"

"Lieutenant, let me tell you this: if you put a loud toy poodle in a room full of pit bulls, the toy poodle still won't know he's not a pit bull until he finds himself in a pit bull's stomach."

Captain Hamilton sighed.

"Captain Lee was not in the mood for it today," he said. "He's normally not quite that growly, but he just wasn't in the mood for it today. He is the one about to get ill over all this, not Captain Bragg."

By this time, they were at Lieutenant O'Reilly's car.

"Be careful on the road, young man – I'll see you after the first shift tomorrow."

"Yes, sir – I'll be praying!"

"Please and thank you!"

On Saturdays, the Tinyville police force ran a split shift, which essentially meant the captain covered the office the first half of the day, and Lieutenant O'Reilly covered the second half. Off he drove, and the captain doubled back to the bar instead of going to his truck right away.

Captain Lee had not come out into the parking lot. The Big Loft officer, although he had Saturday off, was not the kind of man who under normal circumstances lingered at a bar – or anywhere, not in his youth and then really not after West Point, Special Forces, and JAG. Like his cousin, he was one of those men who did what he needed to do and then disappeared into his privacy – except that he was much more of a loner, not having the robust family life Captain Hamilton had enjoyed over the same 23 years of their service.

Captain Lee's blood pressure was also subject to huge spikes, and his cousin had seen his veins swelling up at table. Although the Big Loft captain took excellent care of his body and took his medications dutifully, there were certain triggers and situations that were beyond preventative reach – and the blood pressure was not the only life-threatening problem.

Captain Lee was on the bar side of the bar, at the bar, the bartender making him a drink to order: a triple-strength virgin mojito. That is, a limeade, with three limes and triple mint in the glass – enough potassium and menthol in that to knock that pressure spike down in a hurry. That and some blackstrap molasses, and it was done. He paid the bartender and tipped him well, and then looked at his watch as he began to drink down his virgin mojito. Captain Hamilton knew that the other captain was counting his own heart rate. He could hear what was about to kill him, and was going to listen to it settle all the way back down to safe levels – or at least safe enough for him to go get more advanced medical help.

The bartender returned for the empty glass, three minutes later.

"How was it, Captain Lee?"

"Life-saving. Thank you very kindly."

"If it's that good I ought to try it."

That was Captain Hamilton, who cut his way with a smile through several good-looking women who were looking over Captain Lee with no idea of what was going on, and sat down by his cousin.

"Coming right up!" the bartender said, and went to go get more limes.

"You know, Harry," Captain Hamilton said, "that traffic going into Big Loft on a night like this must be terrible. Why don't you come south with me to Tinyville, and enjoy the weekend with me and the family?"

"I wasn't going back to Big Loft tonight anyhow, Ham."

"That's my whole point, Harry. I know what happens when you get like this. I'd be sick about the whole thing too if I could afford to be, but I've got a big bunch of reasons named Hamilton that I can't, and you need to borrow them for the weekend too."

"I'm tired, Ham. I'm tired of this name I have and what I look too much like, I'm tired of Virginia, I'm tired of the memories of things we've had to do in order to serve this country that just never learns, I'm tired of it, Ham. I do not want to be here any more, and I just don't know how much longer I can take this mess."

"That's right, which is why you are coming home with me."

Like many members of his family, Captain Lee was subject to deep depression, compounded by PTSD – a dangerous problem for a man who needed to take meticulous care of himself. Captain Hamilton understood it, and just grabbed hold of his loner cousin when necessary.

"I've got the chains – put your car in neutral, and I'll tow it, and you can sit up in the truck with me."

"However you want to do it, Ham."

Twenty minutes later, Captain Hamilton was driving down the road to Tinyville, his cousin at last relaxed enough while listening to Southern Gospel on the radio to go on to exhausted sleep. He had slumped over against the window, and every car light illumined the burden he carried in his handsome and all-too-familiar-looking face. The resemblance was not exact, but it was close enough, growing with age as the black hair turned white, and the sorrow of two wars and a ruined people likewise settled upon him. Only, now, asleep at last, was there at last peace in that face.

"It's easy for him to be tired when he has insomnia half the time, Lord," the captain prayed. "So, I've got two things to figure out. I've got to get Harry the help he needs without taking the work from him that he needs to keep going, and I've got to figure out how to honor that Freedom of Information Act request without blowing the county up. I don't have a clue, Lord, and that's bad for an investigator! I'm just counting on You, to get me and Harry safely home, and to show me what to do next."

Chapter 3: Rest and Review and Decision

Reveille was engraved upon the soul of a 23-year soldier – Major Ironwood Hamilton *never* slept past 5:00am, the bugle no longer necessary. It never had been. He had been getting up early for years before West Point, helping younger siblings get ready for school before getting himself to work and school and then home to do the chores at the house, cook, feed, bathe and help his siblings with homework, get them to bed, and then do his homework and work from home before going to bed …

Every day, he did a little check-in with himself. Was Mrs. Agnes Hamilton beside him? Yes. That meant he was no longer the dutiful eldest brother, filling in a year without any adult over him to raise three siblings. It also meant he wasn't waking up in Iraq or Bosnia or Afghanistan, or Iraq again. What color was the uniform he opened his eyes and saw with the little penlight upon it in the closet? Heather gray – all right, now he was oriented.

Captain Ironwood Hamilton of the police force of Tinyville, VA, carefully began to ease out of bed as always so as not to wake his wife, but she was awake and snaked her arms around him.

"You know what I hate?" she purred in his ear.

"What?" he said.

"The whole thought of you doing your isometric workout in the morning, your sinewy body just gleaming and fresh, and that you'll be dressed and out of here for hours and hours before you get that body back here to me."

"Trying to make sure Ira and Agnew don't get to be the baby twins for long, eh?"

Captain Hamilton was 45, his wife 43. It was not likely that they would have another child, but they had said that when he was 43 and she was 41 ... and twins Ira and Agnew had come along the following year.

"Do you mind?"

"Not if you don't, Aggie."

Nonetheless, the wife knew her husband's routines; she expected him to turn around and wrap his arms around her tightly, and roll over with her in bed for a few moments of passion before the roll was complete and he snapped out of bed from her side. He did not disappoint, and for a few moments they indulged the still-intense hunger between them that had produced 11 children in 23 years. Indeed, he snapped out of bed as she expected, but ... .

"Meet me in the shower at 5:45, and you'll get all the gleaming, steaming, and fresh you want before going back to bed quite happy."

On through the house – since he was the only early Saturday riser, Captain Hamilton looked in on each of his children. Yearling twins Ira and Agnew were each still snoring away in their parents' bedroom, each reaching one adorable little hand out to hold the other's between their beds. Their elder twin sisters Ilene and Allison were also asleep in their room, curled up with their dolls and teddy bears. Their elder twin brothers Orson and Edward were also still asleep in their room, although as usual, the state of their beds suggested the adventures they were having in their dreams.

14-year-old Addison, eldest brother at home, had keen senses and was never happy on a summer Saturday when early light was trying to creep through the windows and his father's footsteps started through the house.

"Come on, Dad, it's Saturday," he moaned as his father opened the door to his room.

"If I didn't hear you say that every week, my Saturday wouldn't start right."

"Daaaaaaaaaaaaaaaaaaaaaaaaaaaaaaaaaaaaaad...."

Eldest sisters at home, 16-year-old twins Agnes and Iris, were still in bed, but Iris, an early riser like her father, greeted him: "G'mornin', Dad."

"G'mornin, Iris," he said with a smile. "Just checking in."

Home from college and happily away from the "madness" below with her attic perch: Adella, 19, still snoring away when her father climbed the ladder and peeked in on her.

Lastly, in the guestroom, also arisen to the internal reveille – was the guest for the weekend, Captain Henry Fitzhugh Lee of the Big Loft police department, known as Cousin Harry in the Hamilton family home. He was doing push-ups, alternating one hand with another.

"Top of the morning, Harry."

"57! 58! Top of the morning – 59! 60!"

All was well in the Hamilton home; Captain Hamilton went through his Saturday workout and then returned to his bedroom and stopped for a moment to just enjoy the sound of running water and the pleasant effect that had on his hearing of his wife's singing voice in the master bathroom ... like a melody played on muted strings, affectionate and alluring. Both of those things appealed to Captain Hamilton, and had for 23 years. She was a wonderful soprano, and he enjoyed routinely helping her find her very highest notes...

6:15am – Captain Hamilton arrived in his kitchen to find Captain Lee doing what he did in the morning: he had put on strong coffee and was drinking it black while scanning the newspapers.

"You know, Harry, you're off on Saturdays, unlike me."

"Sleep and weekends are overrated," said Captain Lee. "I must say I was incredibly tempted, however – that bed in there is not for men trying to maintain evening and morning discipline. It was 5:00 before I knew what happened, and I was so comfortable I almost didn't get up."

"Anything interesting in the news?"

"The sheriff's department is trying to work out who is responsible for an outbreak in cow-tipping."

"Ah, summertime in rural Virginia."

"So, what do small-time police forces do on Saturday, in addition with helping to catch cow-tippers and crop thieves?"

"Technically, we are on call for any needs across the county as supplemental to the county forces, as you are in Big Loft, but I personally prefer have the office phone forwarded to my cell phone for part of the shift, and get out into the town and see what is going on. Not today, though; I have been and will be office-bound, using the greater quiet of Saturday to deal with the matters that fall under that Freedom of Information Act request."

Captain Lee drained his coffee cup.

"I suppose I could be more useful helping you than sitting around here."

"Harry, it is all right for you to just enjoy the company of my family."

"In my state of mind, it is not likely that they would enjoy my company."

"Harry, where there's a will, there's a way."

Captain Lee's grave face softened a little.

"Have you taken your blood pressure yet today, cousin?"

"Back at normal, thank you for asking."

He paused a moment, then added, "Thank you, Ham, to you and your family. I am very grateful, although it is hard to see it because I am very troubled."

"I get it, Harry. You know I understand."

"I know you do," he said. "I just can't feel it. It is like living in a glass prison; I can see where I want to be, but I can't touch it."

"Yet," Captain Hamilton.

Captain Lee's face brightened almost to the bud of a smile.

"Forever the optimist, Ham."

"It is hard for you to remember it at these times, but you're not always like this, Harry, not even since the wars and JAG. The Lord will bring you out, and we'll be right here beside you while He is bringing. You know that."

The smile at last budded, although it did not quite blossom.

"I do, Ham. I read in my favorites today – Psalms 23, 42, and 116 – and the Spirit of God encouraged me greatly. I am walking through that valley. I've been here before. I know I will come out, although I am weary of the journey. I know that He has carried me when necessary, like last night when He moved my cousin to get me out of Big Loft and then into his truck and then into that guestroom bed."

He paused.

"I suppose I do feel a bit better."

"The Lord does excellent work," Captain Hamilton said. "Speaking of which: ten parts of the handiwork He has permitted my wife and I to contribute our DNA to will be in this kitchen in about two hours along with their mother. This is my day for kitchen patrol."

"My morning cooking skills are limited beyond oatmeal," said

Captain Lee, "but I would be glad to assist you and learn."

"I cook oatmeal on Sundays, with milk and molasses and cinnamon," Captain Hamilton said, "and I have to keep Ira and Agnew from climbing into the pot."

"If you still are using great-aunt Mildred's recipe, I would almost be willing to climb up into that pot with them."

"The pot is big enough, and we would LOVE to see that, Harry – but we all know you are too neat for that."

At last, the grimness was replaced by a soft smile.

"Just a little," he said, "and besides, that would not be a good example for Ira and Agnew."

"You can get kids to eat their veggies in the morning and love them – chop them up fresh and saute them in some good, fresh butter, and then add them to some eggs scrambled with sweet, fresh milk, salt, pepper, and a handful of good cheese. That and Agnes and the crew having foraged half a freezer full of ramps in the spring, and the other half of the freezer being poke already prepared and ready to cook at any time –."

"Poke sallet and ramps on demand … that could make a sick man well!"

Captain Hamilton smiled.

"Why do you think I insisted that you come here? We get *all* the veggies that make a proper Virginian here, three times a day. It's easy to do and you'll love it all!"

The two police captains put on aprons and set to work – the man from Big Loft chopped and otherwise prepped and let the Tinyville native do the actual cooking. The volume alone was impressive: breakfast for at least 13, for as the captain explained, summers could be hard for some of the local families.

"While kids are in school there is free or reduced breakfast and lunch for them, but in this gap before the crops really start coming in, there are always families that are glad to know there is a safe place, on occasion at least, where a good meal is available. Myself and several members of the church I attend provide this ministry of hospitality to our neighbors; the door is always open, and there are always extra seats at the table. God sends us the resources, and the guests, as He sees fit."

Captain Lee paused in his cutting for a long moment, then resumed.

"God is using you here to stop the crime problem before it begins – deprivation and resentment among the young, and then opportunity to lash back, to take – it accounts for so much crime, and yet doesn't happen when people feel like they are a part of a real community, and that someone with more is there to help someone with less."

"I keep telling people: I am a peace officer now," Captain Hamilton said. "Hospitality makes for peace in a community. I am petitioning Lofton County to provide a summer breakfast program, but there is no need for me to wait as long as the family's resources permit us to do this."

"It can hardly make up for the county's neglect of the matter."

"That is not my responsibility. The Lord only asked me to cook for 20, and stay on the county about the issue until a decision is made. Can't solve every problem, can't carry the burden of doing so – the Lord only requires me to do what He tells me to do. He'll take care of the rest."

The rhythm of the chopping again stopped, and then picked up with much greater speed until all the bell peppers and onions were chopped, and then –.

"All done with these – will you excuse me for a few minutes, Ham?"

The voice was choked, though evenly choked.

"Sure, Harry."

Captain Hamilton listened to the orderly step of his cousin go double-time once in the sitting room, and then, the front door opened,

Captain Lee took off at a run to his car, and slammed its door behind him. He was unwilling to disturb his cousins' rest, but Captain Hamilton slid over to pick up the chopped onions and peppers and saw the tears his cousin had quietly been shedding before his emotions overcame him.

"Mild onions, but at last, Lord, I hope You have granted him some understanding, and relief."

In just a few minutes, the sound of a double-time march returned to the house, and then a regular march through the sitting room to the kitchen, and then the orderly step back to the marcher's post. Captain Lee had returned, and began slicing and dicing potatoes like nothing at all had happened. Upon turning around, Captain Hamilton could see that some of the burden had lifted from his cousin's mind and heart, and although he had little to say as the rest of the Hamiltons rolled on into the kitchen for breakfast and began carrying on as a family that big will, he did seem to relax and enjoy it all.

Captain Lee was not so relaxed that he allowed his cousin to slip out to work without him, and Captain Hamilton was glad for his company and assistance in dealing with the grim task of reviewing those troublesome cases that Captain Hamilton had inherited from his predecessors. Captain Lee knew his data like Captain Hamilton knew his, but Big Loft was 35 times the size of Tinyville, so there was much more data, and much more by the way of patterns to discern. On the other hand: Captain Lee was glad to take notes on the process between Captain Hamilton discovering what was going on and his firing of the three remaining staff members who had created that 10 years of misery for 28 percent of Tinyville.

"The police commissioner is likely not considering releasing three out of five officers in Big Loft's police force," Captain Lee said at the end, "but if he were to do so, you have at least given a good framework for such a decision. I imagine that you took a great deal of anger from the townspeople about this."

"Oh, 72 percent of the town and the *Tinyville Times* were quite disconcerted. The calls for the city council and mayor to fire me were both swift and many. However, the city council and the mayor stood by me, and some privately thanked me for taking the heat they could not afford because of election pressures. They know what Lofton County is in for. They want Tinyville steered as clear as possible, in hopes that some big public-private money may come here."

"So that's what's going on," Captain Lee said. "I knew it was about money in Big Loft, but Tinyville is angling for a piece of it – and you know it had to be about money because Big Loft and Tinyville haven't cared about the people involved, ever."

"You know it," Captain Hamilton said. "However, the leadership in Miniopolis, Littleburg, Smallwood, and Shortport did not become aware of the possibility as early as here in Tinyville, and so, they have let this thing run..."

"And, the *Lofton County Free Voice* has come along to expose them before they can now recover," Captain Lee said. "This of course means the situation is more dangerous than we discussed last night. Big Loft doesn't need the money, although it of course wants it. The smaller towns and the county desperately need it. That Freedom of Information Act request stands to mess up the money."

"None of which will have any bearing on my decision on the subject," Captain Hamilton said, with a smile. "We have one good Lord and Master, and His image is not on any dollar bill!"

"Amen, and amen," Captain Lee said, with a soft smile. "Although I am not in decision making capacity in Big Loft, I will also forward some notes and recommendations from our work today, and in that way fully discharge my duty to our Lord, and let the chips fall where they may."

"That's the Spirit, Harry – really!"

The changing of the guard, as it were, occurred at 4:00pm; Lieutenant O'Reilly would come in then and man the post until 10:00pm. Just before 3:30pm, Captain Hamilton at last finished his big sort, and consigned the last of the files back to the file cabinet.

"Whale of a mess," he said as he locked it.

"Be thankful you are in Tinyville," Captain Lee said. "Our whale in Big Loft is at least 35 times bigger."

"Maybe, maybe not," said Captain Hamilton. "The county prosecutor's office is toast, Harry. That's the other challenge on this. I've got 22 cases in there that never, ever should have been tried, much less a conviction obtained. Another 16 cases should be overturned for only slightly less blatant problems. Still 10 more would be harder to convince an appeals judge on, but not so much so. That's 48 cases, basically five a year for all ten years. The only way that kind of thing continually happens is if there is a corrupt prosecutor on top of corrupt police.

"There's still another problem. If I have at least 48 cases in which the wrong men were convicted, that means I have 48 actual criminals out there just wandering around in full freedom, probably still wreaking havoc somewhere. That's what I can't get people to understand, Harry –

when we do the crime of snatching up a Black man, any Black man, to fill out our private prison quota, we are doing a triple injustice. The first crime is against the innocent man and his family. The second crime is against the victims and their family, who think they are getting closure and safety but they are not, and the third crime is against the whole community, not just that of the innocent man, because the real criminal is still out there.

"This also is the reason I cleaned house down here – 48 cases we know were not solved in five years, and the whole lot of them suspect so far as Black people are concerned – take out traffic stops and the like, and that is a whopping *68 percent* of all cases."

Captain Lee considered this, and jumped almost out of his chair.

"I was doing the numbers on Big Loft – and then Lofton County – and then Virginia – and then the nation – Lord God Almighty, what have we been doing, all this time?"

"Great, great evil," Ironwood Hamilton said grimly. "I thank God for every quiet day He permits us, when one considers what He could be doing – and once did, in Virginia, a century and a half ago."

Captain Lee shook his head.

"My Lord, and my God – what have we been doing?" he repeated.

"Mercy, Lord, please continue in Your mercy, or we are lost!"

"That was what you were saying last night, actually, although to a crowd that does not quite see the matter that way."

"Was I?"

"You did such a fine job I really had little to say."

"I was so tired I do not remember – and now I know why. I have investigated many cold cases in Big Loft since coming, as fairly as I can to those who handled those cases before me, yet I have been meeting all kinds of subtle resistance. At first I thought it was because I am obsessively meticulous, but now I think there might be more to it."

"Indeed there might be. Consider: people who frame other people for crimes might indeed do it for racial reasons, but then again, the average person who frames somebody else for a crime is usually covering for his or herself. That's another reason I had to fire three out of four of my remaining lieutenants. Too many thefts, and too little recovery of money and property, and too poor handling of money and property held as evidence!"

Captain Lee's eyes grew wide.

"Work that out mathematically across the county … oh, there's no bottom to it!"

"Yet again, Harry, we can't fix any of that. Today, we got *this* fixed. We've got Tinyville's number: 48 cases that need to be vacated and started over. We ask the Lord for mercy on all of the rest."

Captain Hamilton paused for a long moment.

"Something wrong, Ham?"

"No ... no, but I think I know what I'm going to do with this Freedom of Information Act request now."

"What?"

"Ask for mercy."

Captain Lee smiled.

"The third way... the way of humility."

"Every 154 years, it seems to work for members of our family in Virginia."

"Overdue to be tried anyhow!"

"Here comes O'Reilly – let's get out of here!"

***

Homeward to the Hamiltons, who were in full hue and cry – with school being out, all of the children old enough to work on Ham it Up Jewelry were assisting their mother, and even the four littlest were involved.

Six-year-old sisters Ilene and Allison were showing the different colors and sizes of bead and bangle to their yearling baby brothers Ira and Agnew. Agnew, like his mother, was sharper on colors, and Ira, like his father, on shapes. Both were having a grand time, showing off their piercing treble voices in their excitement as their sisters cheered them for finding the right objects. Addison, who was in charge of the Ham it Up weblog, was getting plenty of hilarious footage to work with there.

Orton and Edward, each 10 years old, had more substantial work: they had the charge of going through all the bulk items the business ordered and sorting them into likely items to go together. The two brothers were very competitive, and vied for delivering the biggest and best sorts to their sisters Agnes and Iris and their mother, who quickly and expertly made intricate jewelry out of them.

Adella, home for the summer, was acting as a model; Addison's other job was to get plenty of beautiful stills of her wearing the finest works the family business had to offer. In this work, Addison also acted as talent scout, and lit right into his cousin Harry as soon as he arrived.

"Oh, hey Cousin Harry – I've been waiting for you to get here. We've got a ton of shots of Dad wearing our new cuff links and tie pins and men's rings, but he's long and loose and we need some stocky-built looks too!"

Captain Lee delayed too long in his confusion, and Agnes, Iris, and Adella came to get him, singing in glorious three-part harmony...

"Oh, we just love Cousin Harry, and we know that he loves us, so we'll doll up our Cousin Harry – folks will go wild about – will not do without – anything that he wears!"

"Your new career may have just found you," Captain Hamilton said with a chuckle as his three eldest daughters and second son led their cousin away.

"I want a cut of the profits, dagblast it!"

But Cousin Harry was laughing as he surrendered.

There was a lot of laughter and fun in the Hamilton house, even as the industry continued by necessity. Mrs. Hamilton's dream of making a product line of necklaces 25 years earlier had blossomed along with the growth of the family, providing necessary income to support its growth. Everyone attended to it, even and especially Captain Hamilton, who at the end of whatever day, still kept track of the books and dealt with suppliers at home and abroad. His eldest son, Ironwood Jr., was streaking through business school owing to the experiences he had as the family business grew up with him, and still pitched in with market research and contacts even as he traveled to study international business.

It was all a blessing, to the captain's thinking; the business had kept a point of common family productivity together wherever and whenever they were apart from each other … which had been often, because of his long military service. Yet he had called every day that he could just to speak with every member of the family, and then, every eight or nine days, no matter what was going on, his wife received his updated input on this, that, and the other thing that continued to help the family business grow with the years. His body had to be absent, a lot. Yet that was the limit, to the best of his ability.

Every now and again, Ironwood Hamilton would sit down by his wife and apply his eye for detail to a design. In his travels he had seen many kinds of fashions; he would sometimes draw from those memories and what his wife had on hand and surprise her with a new idea – so, on this Saturday, he surprised her by sitting down and taking the time to draw out an entire necklace design before going to get dinner warmed up. Moonstones, pink mother-of-pearl covered ovals, 10k gold setting –

"I call it 'steaming and gleaming,' he said, and walked off as his wife laughed behind him and began seeing how the piece might come together.

Before supper the Hamilton eldest girls and son Addison had gotten their Cousin Harry the way they wanted him, and then began the photo shoot, which was difficult to watch without laughing – the rings, the cuff links, the watch chains, the tie pins, the medallions – they kept coming up with things and he kept saying, "Y'all are ridiculous!" and yet and still taking stunning photos, because he had a stunning sense of pose even if it was just his hand, his arm, and his neck.

"This stuff here is gonna go viral!" Addison shouted. "Dad – I need you to put a suit on for a minute, and your black gloves – and think like Cousin Harry when you put 'em on!"

Indeed, Ham it Up would struggle to stay in watch chains after the black-gloved handshakes of Captains Hamilton and Lee, sporting all six watch chains in stock. Addison knew his marketing!

Finally, everything was put away so that the family could enjoy a high-spirited and relaxed supper, and Captain Hamilton noticed that his cousin Harry was quite relaxed and seemed content, and remained so as he joined in the Hamiltons' summertime games on the porch and in the yard as the sun began to set and the lights came on.

"Early to bed, for early to rise –
Must be in Sunday School, no droopy eyes!"

When Captain Hamilton said that, his children groaned, but obediently put everything away and went inside, the older ones helping the younger ones with getting ready for bed while Captain and Mrs. Hamilton tended to the littlest ones. They left their cousin Harry asleep on the porch; he had gotten so relaxed he had nodded off to catch up on missed sleep from the previous week.

"Go on to bed, Aggie," the captain said when Ira and Agnew were at last asleep. "I'll go walk Harry in."

As Captain Hamilton was going, the words for his letter to the *Lofton County Free Voice* came to him, so, he wrote the letter on the porch, sitting in the chair next to his sleeping cousin. A fold of the paper to go into an envelope the next day, and then a gentle half-waking of his cousin – "Harry, you're going to be sore in the morning if you stay asleep on the porch." Thus to watch the phenomenon of the Big Loft cousin still being pretty much asleep, but awake enough to be guided through a number of actions: teeth brushing, changing of clothes, and getting into bed. He would not remember how he got to bed, but he would re-orient in the morning.

Captain Hamilton addressed his letter to the *Lofton County Free*

Voice and then realized he didn't have an address, but thought out how to deal with that on Sunday, and then went and got into bed. He too had his sleep routines, for often it had been physically necessary to get to sleep as quickly as possible … but his favorite routine was to enjoy a sweet, lingering kiss with Mrs. Hamilton and drift off with her in his arms.

Chapter 4: Sunday-Go-To-Meetings

Sunday – everybody was up early getting into their Sunday best, and Captain Hamilton took that day off of his workout to work with some steel-cut oats ... one whole hour of slow-cooking with milk, molasses, cinnamon, cloves, nutmeg, and finished with butter and nuts and dried fruits. It was Sunday breakfast, and yes, Ira and Agnew didn't want to just eat it. They wanted to worship it, as only babies can ... they wanted to rub it all over their bodies and roll around in it and get into the pot if they could.

Everyone enjoyed, including six "extra" children that came over to eat. They were welcomed and served heartily, and enjoyed the company of the Hamilton children before thanking their hosts and going over the fields back to their homes.

Roadside Southern Baptist was just that – just off the old country road between Tinyville and Littleburg, and attracted all the Southern Baptists of those two towns. It was the survivor of both Captain Hamilton's childhood church and the old Southern Baptist Church of Littleburg. When Captain Hamilton remembered all the circumstances of those collapses, it was emotional enough. Yet on this day, in light of the triple miscarriages of justice that had been going on all throughout the county … and how the presumably large Christian presence in Lofton County had restrained so little of that … and *then* to make sense to what he had witnessed growing up and *knew* was off … it was good that it was children's Sunday, and he could focus on all the children instead of looking into the faces old and new, all day long …

There were people in that church he had known all his life, whom he loved … but in thinking of it he had always been drawn to the ones who were not in prominence, or noticed by the prominent, the ones who quietly ministered to everyone around them before, during, and after church … the ones who had looked with kindness on those whom others willfully overlooked … the ones who had suffered for doing so …

"Woody...?"

Captain Hamilton came to himself in tears as the rousing postlude was being played on the old organ. His wife was alarmed because of how rarely her husband showed such emotion in public, or even with the family unless at home in their private world. He and his cousin were not dissimilar in that they showed a marble front that hid deep emotion and deep, deep pain from the world. Captain Hamilton smiled more readily everywhere, but … .

"Would you like to go on a quick drive with me while Sunday dinner on the yard is going on, Aggie?"

"Of course, Woody."

He would tell her. Always and as long as they both lived, he would confide in her, and vice versa. At Roadside's dinners, the Hamilton little ones would be well-supervised both by their elder siblings and church staff, and their parents could have half an hour alone before returning to re-join the fun.

Mrs. Hamilton squeezed her husband's hand, and he smiled, took his handkerchief, and in a few moments was himself again, cheerily greeting and meeting and all the rest. Yet there was a poignancy about it that the more sensitive picked up, and they lingered a moment or two to pray with the captain.

Captain Lee touched Mrs. Hamilton gently on her elbow.

"I don't know if you have noticed," he said, "but your church is splitting before our eyes."

"I see it," Mrs. Hamilton said. "Woody has been saying it never was really together, but, it is close and the Word is preached faithfully by the new pastor – but yes, Harry, I know."

Outside: Cousin Harry distracted Ira and Agnew so their parents

65

could slip away for a little while – and, off they clambered into Captain Hamilton's pickup truck. Mrs. Hamilton could tell her husband was in quite a state because of how he was driving – flirting with breaking the county speed limit, white-knuckled on the steering wheel. His face was drawn – resolve, anger, both? – and only relaxed as they pulled up in front of Emanuel Baptist Church of Tinyville, VA.

Thomas Stepforth Sr., himself in tears, stepped forth with his son's family all around him ... all in tears of joy as they all had been praising the Lord because Major Thomas Stepforth Jr. would be coming home after completing a full 20 years of service – and was retiring, so, home for good! His children, including his eldest son Thomas Stepforth III, were still rejoicing – "Thank you, God – I know You can do anything but fail, because Dad is coming home for good!"

The very last people Mr. Stepforth expected to see walking up on his family in this moment of rejoicing were the Hamiltons. He certainly knew the captain, and was developing a guarded, grudging, but definite respect for him. Mrs. Hamilton he knew from her trips with her littlest children, the same age as his youngest grandchildren – they were often seeing each other, and the New Yorker was forward and friendly and very sweet to his grandchildren.   Mrs. Hamilton was one of those women that, if Mr. Stepforth discovered she was prejudiced, he would actually have been surprised.

Mr. Stepforth noticed that the captain had a letter in his hand, and restrained his surprise when the police officer walked right up with his wife and started greeting the entire family – Mrs. Hamilton knew everybody, and it was a surprisingly pleasant moment of introductions. Mrs. Stepforth Jr. broke the news about Major Stepforth coming home, and Mrs. Hamilton hugged her – "Friend, ask me if I understand your joy!" – and they started bawling all over each other as the littler children danced around them.

Meanwhile, the captain held the letter out to Mr. Stepforth.

"This is my response to the Freedom of Information Act request from the *Lofton County Free Voice*," he said. "I'm comfortable with not knowing the paper's address, and comfortable with not asking you about it. Let them know from me, officially, that I am complying with the request."

Mr. Stepforth jumped.

"You are?" he said.

"I sent it in writing, and they can quote me on it and call me a liar if I don't. I just want to discuss certain details in person. I'm asking you to use your influence to make that personal meeting happen, at a location comfortable to the *Free Voice*. I will make myself available at any time I don't have official business."

"You will?"

"Yes, sir, I will. You, and the *Free Voice,* have my word."

Mr. Stepforth felt like dancing down the stairs like one of the Nicholas Brothers in a tap routine, but he got hold of himself.

"Expect a call from me tonight – and clear your calendar for tomorrow morning."

"I don't have any meetings – that will work."

"Good day, sir."

"Good day, sir."

Victory, yet again; the celebration of the Stepforths trebled with the joy in the heart of the family patriarch, that one of the goals to which he had bent himself since moving to Tinyville, and seeing the plight of the community in which his grandchildren were growing up even as he had, was being met. Things were certainly changing!

"Thou, Lord!" he cried out, and again burst into tears of joy and went on and danced down those stairs with his old tap skills, raising the letter in his hand up to the sky in joyful praise as his family danced around him, after the Hamiltons had gone out of sight.

The Hamiltons were rolling down the old country roads back to their church ... only when they were out of the truck and walking back toward the churchyard did Mrs. Hamilton notice the slight tremor in her husband's hands.

"Woody ... ?"

"I've just surrendered, Agnes, to that Freedom of Information Act demand, and will be asking for merciful terms tomorrow."

"Oh, Woody ... ."

"That doesn't bother me. That is the way the Lord is leading me. What bothers me is what we are about to go do, in light of how most of them would react to what I have just done. If I didn't know them well enough to know most of them would gladly hang me in the churchyard, that would be one thing, but I *know these people.* They are *my people,* my kindred, my neighbors, my culture, and to think that after 150 years of this region being in the Bible Belt, I *know* that most of them would hang me for following the Lord's leading *and* the law of the land. I know this. Yet I came back here. Working here I can handle. Acting like we are worshiping the same God? That is getting very difficult. It has been very difficult since both churches split, and my family fell through the cracks. It is now becoming nearly intolerable."

"The wheat and the tares, Woody, the wheat and the tares ... they have to grow up together," Mrs. Hamilton said. "However, if you need to find another church to be at peace, I will follow you wherever you wish to go."

Captain Hamilton turned to his wife with a smile.

"I know. You came with me here. You've gone around the country with me. That, I'm not worried about, yet."

He drew her close, and murmured in her ear.

"What I'm really thinking of is something one of our neighbors who is feeding our neighbors in need has said ... it may be time to found a new church in Tinyville, where God's children in Tinyville can worship in spirit in truth together."

Mrs. Hamilton gasped from surprise, but then put her mouth by her husband's ear.

"Well, if we're going to get hung so God can get the glory, let's do it BIG, Ironwood. I'm with you. If we decide to do it, I'm with you 100 percent."

She noticed immediately; the tension went out of her husband's body at that point. They returned to the churchyard after that, the secret between them steadying them both as they met and greeted and chatted with folks Captain Hamilton knew, all too well.

Captain Hamilton's cousin was having a far better time, having been led by Ira and Agnew Hamilton (figuratively speaking) into a world of little ones who just adored his singing and his willingness to play their games. The church's single women from ages 25 to 50 were also slowly closing ranks on his position, drawn by his good looks, his lack of a ring on the third finger of his left hand, and his utter giftedness with children.

"He doesn't look depressed now," Mrs. Hamilton said, with a chuckle.

"If he's not careful," said Captain Hamilton, "some poor girl will be fooled like you were."

"And so he will get cured!" Mrs. Hamilton said triumphantly. "That man needs a helpmeet along with the right therapy and medical adjustments – he needs the right helpmeet to help him get the most of what he already has, and motivate him to get on off into it!"

"It's not going to be as easy for Harry," Captain Hamilton said.

"It will be if God bring him the one meant for him, as I was meant for you. I'm praying for it to happen!"

"Well, keep praying for it – the crowd is growing so it must be working!"

Yet Captain Lee waded through that crowd of hopeful ladies like they were not even there, when all was done – he greeted, he met, and walked on. He made a comment to Captain Hamilton that explained the situation to Mrs. Hamilton, when Captain Hamilton had shared his outreach to Mr. Stepforth.

"You are walking a hard path, Ham, but how the Lord has blessed you, in that you do not walk alone. Yet your courage even in that is above what most men could endure, in that you have dared to lead another down this dangerous path with you. I admire you without ever thinking I could meet you in courage."

"Well, here's another chance to build some courage – Mr. Stepforth has made the connection, and the editor-in-chief and a reporter from the *Lofton County Free Voice* are coming to formalize my surrender tomorrow morning. Think you can talk your superiors in Big Loft into letting you peek in on the meeting?"

"They will doubtless be interested in hearing how you handle the paper's representatives, although I think they would be disappointed in your approach," said Captain Lee. "However, life is full of disappointments!"

"Isn't it, now – I'll be disappointed if I don't see you at 10:45."

"I'll try not to let you down, Ham."

Captain Lee drove off, looking much better than he had the day before, and the Hamiltons went on home to enjoy the rest of another fun-filled evening.

Sunday night was stay-up-late day in the summer, and after preparing for bed, folks worked on or played on or talked on into the night until they were caught nodding. On this night, Mrs. Hamilton could gauge how her husband was feeling by what he did; he sat down right by her at her desk, and drew designs for her while letting Ira and Agnew climb up and down and show what they were also drawing. His designs that evening were open and spacious ... the tension of the day had left him. They sat and discussed them while their children finally wound on down, and then, when everyone else had been put to bed or had gone to their rooms, the parents at last went to bed, and Mrs. Hamilton felt peace in her husband's body as he drew her to him.

"Good night, Woody ... I'm already praying about your meeting tomorrow ..."

"I know. I love you. Thank you. Good night, Aggie."

"I love you too, Woody. Good night."

A sweet kiss, and Mrs. Hamilton felt her husband's body settle into sleep.

Chapter 5: Confrontation and Concerning Words

How it could be that the African in America was considered less than human, or less than handsome, eluded the mind of Ironwood Hamilton, never more than when looking upon men such as James Varick IV, the editor-in-chief of the *Lofton County Free Voice*. Certainly he had all the features Southern white men had been taught to despise – skin the color of glowing coal, black and yet luminous; broad forehead, dark eyes, broad nose, full, heavy lips. He also had the features those same white men also had always feared; he was six feet five, and every inch a fit giant of about 45 years of age. In a physical contest without weapons, he might do as he pleased with nearly any opponent. He also had what Southern white men hated the most in black men: brimming masculine confidence, as befit a man walking into the enemy's headquarters to receive the enemy's surrender. He was the walking embodiment of the dashing of the Founders' plans for black men, and the failure of their Confederate sons to secure those plans – Mr. James Varick IV was every inch a man, and his presence forced one to acknowledge him as such.

At Mr. Varick's side was another man, perhaps 15-20 years younger, but also impressive – six feet tall, lithe as a graceful bronze statue, with similar features – a relative, perhaps – but with a more pointed make. He also brimmed confidence, but also something more … intense anger, of a much higher order that Captain Hamilton had encountered in Mr. Thomas Stepforth Sr. at their first meeting.

The younger man was the embodiment of the hate that 400 years of hate, and ten years of injustice to be discussed that day, had created. His lip curled in contempt as he looked on Captain Hamilton, and still more as his eye registered the all-too-familiar features of Captain Lee, who had returned to Tinyville to observe on behalf of Big Loft and Lofton County. His fist clenched, as if every statue of Robert E. Lee that could not be knocked down in Virginia might instead be at least given a black eye if he could but get to Captain Lee's quite similar face. However, Captain Lee ignored him with marble precision after looking him over once, which angered him even more.

"Good morning, Mr. James Varick IV and Mr. Nathan Turner," Captain Hamilton said.

"Good morning, Captain Hamilton and Captain Lee," the two men answered.

"Rest yourselves and sit down wherever you like – would you like coffee, tea, orange juice...?"

"While we appreciate the hospitality, Captain," Mr. Varick said, "we have a paper to get together. Shall we get down to business?"

"Very well; as you like," Captain Hamilton said.

Mr. Varick pulled out his digital recorder, turned it on, and put it on Captain Hamilton's desk as Mr. Turner pulled out his notebook.

"Of course we are on the record, Captain."

"Of course, Mr. Varick."

Captain Hamilton pointed out his digital recorder, already on (and Mr. Turner started slightly), and then inclined his head toward Captain Lee, who was taking notes as well.

"Write what you will about me," Captain Hamilton said with a cool smile, "but you won't be able to say I don't believe in equality of access to information, and of keeping good records on all sides."

Mr. Turner bristled visibly, but Mr. Varick smiled back.

"Given your record since you have taken over, I expected no less from you, Captain. But speaking of equal access to information, we are here to receive your response to the *Lofton County Free Voice's* Freedom of Information Act request, with any details you might find of importance."

Captain Hamilton reached into his desk's bottom drawer, and pulled out five thick folders.

"These are copies of the reports and cases involving African Americans in Tinyville for the last ten years. Each folder holds two years of data. Nothing has been redacted or withheld. I have added an index, and I have sorted them based on type of incident for ease of use."

Mr. Varick and Mr. Turner received the files, and took their time examining them in detail. Captain Hamilton watched their expressions: surprise at the amount of data released, anger, sorrow, surprise, chagrin, even a sad chuckle from Mr. Varick with a head shake, and then surprise as they realized – .

"This appears to be complete," Mr. Varick said.

"It is," Captain Hamilton said. "Given that you have more staff to devote to exploration of the data than I have, there may be things you discover that I am not yet aware of, but I stand ready at any time to answer any questions you may have about the data."

Mr. Turner had been carrying a big suitcase; at a nod from Mr. Varick, the reporter put the files into the suitcase and snapped it shut.

"I also have something else of interest to you," Captain Hamilton said as he opened the top drawer of his desk. "This is a formal apology from me, on behalf of this department, for the injustices committed against the African American community in Tinyville and its surroundings in the last ten years I am aware of."

Mr. Varick started; Mr. Turner scarcely restrained his lip from curling.

"Are the three lieutenants responsible for much of the data you have turned over on administrative leave, or fired?" Mr. Turner asked.

"Fired," Captain Hamilton said. "Owing to the size of the town, I am captain, chief, and commissioner. My personnel decisions can only be overturned by the city council or the mayor, and they have declined to overturn the firings."

"Are you aware of the county's attempts to reassign them to other positions in law enforcement in the county?"

"I am."

"And your position on that is?"

"My position is that men who so clearly have no interest in the proper working of law and justice should never be allowed any position of community responsibility and authority again until they have brought forth fruits worthy of repentance. My position is known in every law enforcement office in the county where these men have applied."

"Is there data supporting the prosecution of these men for criminal misconduct?"

"There is."

"What have you done in that direction?"

"I have submitted the appropriate evidence to the county prosecutor, with the supporting evidence. The county prosecutor has declined the case."

Mr. Turner gritted his teeth, but subsided as Mr. Varick gave him a concerned but cautioning look, and then spoke.

"Is there anything else that you can do?"

"Not in that direction, no. But I have another idea, and I hope that you will consider assisting me with it."

Mr. Varick raised a salt-and-pepper eyebrow, even as Mr. Turner's eyes lit up and his face clearly said, "NO!"

"In those files you will discover at least 48 cases in which it is very likely that those committed should have their convictions vacated and their cases dismissed. My request is that you will not publicize the details of those cases in mass."

"What!" Mr. Turner said. "The most damning thing on your accursed travesty of a department, and you want it withheld!"

"Let's hear him out," Mr. Varick said. "We can always say no,

Nathan – we already have the data."

"Then why are we wasting our time with this – this –!"

He was so angry he could no longer speak, and subsided as Mr. Varick spoke again.

"I am really in consensus with Mr. Turner," he said, "but, we'll hear you out."

"When you have examined the data, you will observe what I observe; there are at least 48 men in jail or prison who should be exonerated. I have already been in contact with Virginia's branch of the Innocence Project up at the University of Virginia at Charlottesville, and apprised them of as much of the situation as I can, within the constraints of my position. I am willing to support your efforts, with theirs, to have the men in question exonerated; I will cooperate fully.

"However, with the exoneration of the innocent we surely must see that 48 people, or at least enough to account for those cases, have been living free in the community for at least ten years. My interest as police captain is to bring the truly guilty parties to justice. I have already begun my investigations in that direction. If you were to release all the information about those 48 cases, the truly guilty parties will know they are again in danger, and will destroy what little evidence remains to

81

convict them, or flee."

"That's your problem, Hamilton," Mr. Turner gritted. "It's your problem that your former colleagues thought it was a good idea to put innocent men and their families through ten years of suffering and let the guilty run free. We want full exoneration in the eyes of the law and the community for the innocent; we don't care about embarrassing you and your department."

"With all due respect, Mr. Turner, that is very short-sighted," Captain Hamilton said. "Your community is part of Tinyville. It has suffered from further crimes, and likely lost more innocent men to jail and prison owing to the actions of people who were not caught and were thus emboldened to continue their behavior. Assuming they are moving around the county, the truly guilty are likely also responsible for crimes that have created occasion for false arrests elsewhere in the county – and although in Tinyville I follow the most stringent standards of investigation, I cannot do anything outside Tinyville unless called by the county to do so."

"He's got a point," Mr. Varick said.

"You can't be serious, Uncle!" Mr. Turner cried.

"I'm not asking you to suppress the information permanently,"

Captain Hamilton said. "My plan is to work these cases as best I can such that by the time you and the Innocence Project have worked to free the innocent men, I can quickly catch up those who should have been in prison all this time. If I can't, I'll take the humiliation of not being able to provide that element of full exoneration that only I can: the capture and presentation to the force of law and justice of the truly guilty, so that the last of the stigma that the victims and their families and the region would otherwise still attach to the exonerated can fall away."

"In other words, drip the information on each individual case slowly, so that the guilty parties don't know you are coming."

"Yes," Captain Hamilton said. "There has been a triple injustice done: to the innocent men, their families, and their portion of Tinyville's community; to the families of the victims, who think they have received justice but have not; and to the community at large because my department chose to indulge its racism instead of bringing the guilty to face justice. It is my opinion that as much should be repaired as possible, and if you will help me, I think we can."

"No!" Mr. Turner thundered. "You are not going to co-opt the *Lofton County Free Voice* to your ideas of justice! I won't stand for it! We are not going to make yet another unholy alliance with a system that has done nothing but work to destroy Africans in America for 400 years! No! No! NO!"

The anger and the pain upon Mr. Turner's face was vivid as he rose from his chair, his fists raised as if he would dash the life from Captain Hamilton.

"Sit down, Nathan," Mr. Varick said, through gritted teeth. "We're in a police station and you've lost track of one of them – sit down and control yourself!"

Indeed, Captain Lee had drawn his weapon, although he had not taken the safety off yet.

Mr. Turner regained his tactical awareness, and sat down, but his seething rage had only changed position.

"The blood of my brother and many others already cry out from the soil of Tinyville to the Lord against this department!" he cried. "But you already should know that, Captain Hamilton – do you think your miserable paddy-rolling department deserves any cooperation from us? We don't want to help you work your system – it has never worked for us! You deserve *nothing* of our assistance – all that your people did not take from us by force in 246 years of slavery, 100 years of Jim Crow, and 60 years of permitted criminal misconduct, you may *never willingly have!* Do you understand me? You deserve *nothing!"*

"I know that," Captain Hamilton said, very quietly.

"What did you say?" Mr. Turner gritted.

In the next instant, you could have heard a pin drop.

"I said, I know that I deserve nothing, as the head of this department. Mercy is always undeserved. But that is what I am asking for, on behalf of the whole community we have to live in. There is no other organization beside this department that can go track down the truly guilty. There is no guarantee that is can be done; there is only a decent chance. You do not have to give it to me. I, and this department, do not deserve it. I am asking for mercy on behalf of the entire town, although much of it has been merciless to you and yours for 400 years, and I submit that the mercy you show will also be of great benefit to you and yours, in both greater public safety and the completion of the work of exoneration for the innocent."

Silence, for a long time, and then Mr. Varick spoke in a calm, authoritative voice.

"The *Lofton County Free Voice* has a team of editors, and you are not nor will you ever be on it, Captain," he said. "But neither are you, Nathan, although of course your opinion holds much more weight with the team.   The deciding factor must be the greater good of the constituency we are primarily concerned with. The 72 percent of this town you represent by your heritage has made a hard bed for itself with its injustices, Captain, and it is not our primary concern to help you solve that problem.   However, we are interested in the full exoneration of the innocent, and in public safety for the town and county because we live here and are going to take an even more active role in both in the future. Therefore, the editorial staff will consider your request."

"That is all I ask," Captain Hamilton said.   "Thank you.   I will pursue the 48 cases in any event, and it is also in my interest, because in the interests of justice, to see the innocent parties fully exonerated."

"You shall be given plenty of occasion to assist with that, Captain," said Mr. Varick, "and we will be right along with you to witness it, and report on it."

"I expect no less, gentlemen," said Captain Hamilton.   "You have certainly impressed me with the investment you are making in the discourse and direction of this town's affairs."

Mr. Varick smiled thinly.

"We are 28 percent of the population of Tinyville, 39 percent of Lofton County.   We are delayed in making that impression, but not denied. We do not intend to ever be denied again."

"You have certainly impressed me with the fact, gentlemen."

Mr. Varick reached over and turned off his digital recorder, and Mr. Turner completed his notes. Mr. Varick stood first, then Captain Hamilton, then Captain Lee, and then Mr. Turner, who put his notebook in the suitcase before moving.

"Good morning, gentlemen," Captain Hamilton said.

"Good morning, Captains," the two news men said.

They strode off, data in hand, a passionate discussion commencing when they thought they were out of earshot – but not quite.

Passing up the street, coming also to see Captain Hamilton, was Captain Bragg, apparently in the middle of a conversation –

"Smash those fools like rusted tin cans, now that we've got a line on them –."

He had walked into the middle of the office while saying that, and then jumped – "Oh, sorry, y'all, on the phone – hey, let me get back to you on that. Thanks."

And he reached up and touched his Bluetooth, and shut it off – almost. The little blue light at the top kept blinking, a phenomenon that seemed to fascinate Captain Lee so much that it attracted Captain

Hamilton's gaze as well.

"I was passing through on my way up to Big Loft and I thought I'd stop by and let you know where I am on this whole Freedom of Information Act foolishness, Captain Hamilton, but wasn't that some folks from that rag now, just leaving you?"

"Yes."

"Got them arguing among themselves with the line you took, I take it – good job! A little more of that from you, and we'll be able to get this whole mess settled down, combined with what I am doing."

"Which is?"

"I've been in the county and Big Loft's ear all morning, and I've got my people going through the records. We've found out some things: old Angler [Captain Angler of Smallwood] was right. There's enough data to drown a small paper – we just have to do the sort so the things we want hidden stay hidden. Everybody already knows there's racial profiling, and a majority of the people of this county support it – so, let the rag whine, and blow off steam until there's some other news for them to focus on!"

Captain Bragg's blue eyes gleamed brightly, by contrast to the cooler light in Captain Hamilton's eye, and voice.

"I agree with the idea of a full release, with some tweaks to the methodology."

"Well, of course you do!" Captain Bragg said. "Any sensible person – anyway, we are all following Angler's lead in the next few days, so if you could go ahead and get moving, Hamilton –."

"Consider it done, Captain Bragg."

Captain Bragg smiled gently.

"Do you know what I like about you, Captain Hamilton?" he said.

"No."

"You've been home three months, and you didn't come home presuming to leadership because you've been around the world and done this and that. Even though some of your ideas are ridiculous in terms of how to deal with the minorities in this town and county, at least you work with those who know better in a productive way! You are really good at facilitating and working with those who have had to hold the line for law and order down here while you have been away. You don't presume to leadership where you don't deserve it and haven't earned it."

"In my experience," Captain Hamilton said, "time and circumstances reveal the quality of a leader, and he will rise to the top in his time."

"Exactly. As men of thought go, Hamilton, you have a lot of good sense. I'm considering your release done, and I'm off to Miniopolis. Two days from now, think of that whole rag's staff, all sitting in one place, overwhelmed by that load of kindling we're giving them, waiting on the next news – oh, it's a thought that warms the heart!"

Off he went, having never even acknowledged Captain Lee, who in turn never acknowledged him, but persisted in working on his notes until Captain Bragg turned his back. Captain Lee noiselessly rose and followed Captain Bragg into the street, and watched, until … .

"Captain Bragg is parked around the far corner," he said.

"I'm glad you thought of all that," Captain Hamilton said as he at last turned off his recorder.

"Why not?" Captain Lee said grimly. "He may indeed have hit on a solution to several things of your interest, and that of this county."

Captain Lee went over to the copy machine and made copies of his notes to leave with the Tinyville captain, and the Tinyville captain turned his attention to the report Lieutenant O'Reilly had left about his call that morning, and the update he had just sent in. When he looked up, Captain Lee was standing at his desk, his normally composed face covered with emotion.

"I would applaud you – I would cheer you for how you have conducted yourself this morning, except that I know that it is the Spirit of God within you that has led you through this morning in this amazing way, and Who must get the glory for what is done and yet to be done!"

"Amen," Captain Hamilton said. "I was just thinking the same thing. All praises and glory to God, Who has led me through this treacherous morning and will lead through the hard days that are to come!"

Captain Hamilton stood and reached his hand out to his cousin, who shook it, and then pulled him into his embrace.

"Oh, Ham, if I had given up at any point, I would not have been here this day with you!"

"I keep telling you, Harry – God wants you here, because there is a lot we can and must still do! Survivor's guilt is a tough thing, but we survived Five Bright Nine because our work wasn't done. Our buddies went to their reward – but we're not finished yet!"

"I see it, Ham – and I'm starting to feel it, just today, here with you. Oh, thank God, thank You, that You never have put up with this Lee's follies any more than You ever did any another! Thank You! Thank You!"

Captain Lee lifted his hands heavenward for just a few moments in worship and praise, and then calmed down.

"I'm due back at my desk at 2:00 – care for some lunch, now?"

"Lieutenant O'Reilly is bringing it, with a great story that will cheer us right up –."

"I'm here – and I solved the cow-tipping case!" cried the young lieutenant as he burst in, all fresh air and blue skies and knowing nothing about the heavy work that had been and was still to come in that office.

"And we want to hear all about it!" Captain Hamilton said as Captain Lee smiled and relieved the younger man of his bags of lunch.

After lunch, Captain Hamilton walked his cousin to his car.

"Pull out all you can about theft and grand theft incidents from the data covered by the Freedom of Information Act request," he said, "and send me a good summary. I'll do the same for you. My thinking is that the data will suggest both possible answers and good questions."

"It is going to be interesting, getting those questions asked and answered," Captain Lee said.

"Oh well," said Captain Hamilton. "We survived Five Bright Nine, Harry. By comparison, this will be a Sunday School picnic."

Captain Lee laughed from surprise.

"Forever the optimist!"

"One of us has to be. Virginia already has Big Pappa glowering everywhere, his stone face unable to smile ever again. Terrible thing they've done to him, in making him an idol. And then I have to get you sold on smiling again – so yes, one of us has to be an optimist!"

Captain Lee laughed until he cried.

"Let me out of here before you have me running off the road, laughing! You're a menace to all depression, Ham!"

"Unrepentant and unashamed," Captain Hamilton said after he closed his cousin's car door and his cousin rolled down the window. "Stay in prayer, and try to get me that information no later than tomorrow afternoon."

"You'll have it tonight, Lord willing. I'll see you later."

"Oh – you're coming back to the meetings!"

"I do listen to you, Ham, even if I don't always show it."

Chapter 6: The Calm Between the Storms

Monday – come rain or come shine, in coordination with understanding friends and relatives, Captain and Mrs. Hamilton went up to Roanoke, VA for two things: a dinner date, and a support group for veterans and their wives at Roanoke's Veteran's Administration Hospital. The order of those two things depended on how Captain Hamilton felt. If he were relaxed, they would have early dinner, go to the group, and go get dessert or maybe catch a movie. If he were not relaxed, the group would come first, and afterward he would feel well enough to go enjoy dinner.

Captain Hamilton carried a lot of tension quite well to externals; the average person observing him would never have known the difference between a day when he felt relaxed or one which he was very stressed. He had carried heavy responsibility since the age of 14; after 31 years, he could stay calm and functional in situations in which other people would be in a blubbering heap. Yet no one could do this forever, and for Captain Hamilton, the support group was a necessary time for him to be in a place in which he did not have to provide the structure and the resources for things to go, and where he could discuss the events that had scarred him and how they affected his life and that of his family.

Mrs. Hamilton found the meetings difficult and wonderful at the same time. The stories were hard, and the emotions were harder – the fact that her husband was right at home with all of it was strange until he decided to share his stories … both Special Forces and JAG had provided him with some truly wrenching decisions, and memories. Rarely did he repeat a story: he had so many. She loved him all the more because he gallantly and cheerfully went about loving and serving their family even while in so much hidden pain that she didn't know about.

Mrs. Hamilton knew about plenty of the pain, of course – he told her about his meeting that morning with Mr. Varick and Mr. Turner of the *Lofton County Free Voice*, of the reactions that he had restrained, and of his fears, fears he expounded on with the group:

"People don't understand when they work with high-functioning PTSD survivors – any kind of close physical threat will trigger the old reactions. I look normal: I'm not, and sometimes, it's a curse to the people around me.

"I had some citizens today nearly get themselves into a cross between me and another like me with the same issues. I never should have let them sit so close, should have rearranged the room the moment I realized one of them was so angry. But I can't think of everything in advance. I'm only human, no matter what angel or devil you've heard of from your friends in Lofton County. The meeting was going to be tense anyhow, and I was trying to keep it from going off the rails. It went off anyhow, and I was instantly about to be in hand-to-hand combat in Afghanistan, programmed to kill a man in thirty ways. He would have been dead before either of us knew what had happened, but for the grace of God that has allowed me to get into and stay in both support groups and therapy to help me turn off those triggers."

That other veteran spoke out.

"I was the other veteran," said Colonel Henry Fitzhugh Lee, "serving in my capacity as police captain at Big Loft. Major Hamilton would never have named me, but here there is no need for the secret. As y'all know, Major Hamilton is my cousin, and he and I served together in Special Forces. I watched him once break everything but a man's neck and back in ten seconds – even in the moment of combat, he would not kill a man unless absolutely necessary. Thus he was known as 'Colonel Lee's more humane adjutant.'

"I work in Big Loft's police department, but not on street duty. I work complex investigative problems involving data and cold cases, of which Big Loft has many. He is the one you want out with the hysterical public. Not me. He is right when he describes the danger those citizens were in. I would have shot them both and never thought twice about it if I had assessed that the citizens in question were truly a threat. They weren't. They are still alive this evening. The grace of God, for me and them, was that He showed me they were just angry, not really intending harm to my adjutant and dear friend.

"Major Hamilton is not a killer, although he has killed when necessary and only when necessary. He is blessed to be good at *not killing*. Not I. I am a killer. I am very, very good at what I do. I have killed, many times, on behalf of my units, and regret nothing except that at Five Bright Nine, there was not even enough killing to be done to have saved more of my men. Had there been, I would have gladly done it. I know that I am at home, stateside, far from the scenes of battle that the major and I shared. Yet what has changed in me may never change back. All I can do is walk with the Lord, and seek the help I need – and, learn to do as Major Hamilton said, and assess situations that may trigger me so as to remove myself from them in advance."

"That's what we are all here to help each other learn," said Colonel John Parker, the facilitator of the Roanoke group. "We all have different practices in terms of faith or philosophy, but what we can all learn together is now how to learn how to wage peace. War is natural to proud and selfish people, but there are skills to get good at it. We can also get good at peace; there are skills and I see both of you managed to apply them in the nick of time. Thank you both for sharing."

Mrs. Hamilton noticed that her husband had broken into a soaking sweat as he relived his day, while his cousin was much calmer – that marble front still held up. The difference between them was thus starkly illustrated.

"Thank you for talking me into making this Monday meeting, Ham; we needed that," Captain Lee said to his cousin after the meeting ended.

"Oh, I know that – that's why I'm here every week wondering if you are going to show up half the time, Harry."

"I give you my word that I am going to be faithful weekly from now on – things are getting too serious out here, and in this next week, we shall have to be prepared in both arts."

"Peaceful as we can be, warlike as we must."

"That's what you were always my humane adjutant, Ham – and now I will be your adjutant, and we pray that we can wrap all this up without too much bloodshed as *peace officers,* after all."

"You know," Captain Hamilton said, "I wonder if why things stayed so bad after the Civil War is that there was no cultural commitment to transition back to peace."

Captain Lee shook his head, his face sad.

"Victory, defeat, and peace are three completely different things. I don't think this nation has ever pursued the third. When have we embraced the things that go with peace? Contentment with the things that we already possess – no. Contentment with our lot without envious comparison with others – no. Accepting life's ups and downs, and especially the downs, while accepting full responsibility for all of it – no. Accepting the fact that we have been wrong, from sea to shining sea, in believing and acting as if certain groups of people only existed and still exist to be ground up at our pleasure and for our profit– no. Repenting of said wrong: no. There can be only two kinds of peace for people eaten up with wanton materialism: the first is that they mature past that, and the second is that they die, thereby providing peace for their victims."

"Well, that's harsh, Harry."

"You're the humane one, Ham. I'm not. We had better pray now that the people we have to track down in the next three to five days don't make me have to show the difference."

Mrs. Hamilton shivered at all this talk, but she accepted her husband

and his veteran associates for who they had been made to be on behalf of the United States, and just started praying.

Captain Lee looked over at Mrs. Hamilton, and smiled gently.

"You see why I resist your efforts at matchmaking, my dear Agnes? Your husband is still the same kindhearted man he always was. I know that I am not."

"Yes, you are," Captain Hamilton said. "You didn't become a killer because you loved to kill, Harry. You became a killer like we all did, because there was no other way. Just because you were proficient at it, just because you were able to raise it to an art that saved the lives of many of those you were sworn to protect, doesn't make you any better or worse than the rest of us. You're a brilliant defensive tactician, like Big Pappa. The tragedy is that you both have been put to the same use, and you are even better at it."

"Which is the struggle," Captain Lee said. "That is the struggle."

"I know, Harry. Take it back to the Lord in prayer, especially in these next few days."

Captain Lee and the Hamiltons parted, and Mrs. Hamilton got up her courage.

"Woody, I've never asked you about Five Bright Nine, but ... ."

"A lot of it is classified, so I can't tell you about that part," Captain Hamilton said. "Suffice it to say that Unit 6 was put on a mission that somebody above us bungled badly in terms of strategy. Harry realized it five minutes too late, but also five minutes before we were going to be set upon by a force ten times our size. Harry knew what direction they were coming from, and that they would be overconfident.

"I'm here, Agnes, in full possession of life and limb. That ought to tell you plenty, but I'll go a little further: there were nine members of Unit 6. Five of us walked away, carrying two of our brothers to safety. Harry mourns his lost two, and the 80 men we killed there on his orders – and the 50 more we killed in achieving our objective, reversing the ambush on those that sent it since we knew they expected that their ambush would have destroyed us.

"Harry is *brilliant,* Agnes. They lured him back here on account of "cold cases" – they knew in Big Loft that they had a problem 35 times the one in Tinyville, and they wanted to put someone in there with a reputation for handling big data problems. Harry was able to do that in JAG as well: give him 30, 40, or 100 data points, and he can figure out what a team of investigators should be doing to get things done. Yet Five Bright Nine haunts him. He mourns our dead, he is furious with the system that allowed our superiors to avoid responsibility for their deadly bungling, and he fears the living – *himself.*"

"Oh, Woody … that explains so many things about him."

"One other thing. Harry absolutely detests people who bungle and don't take responsibility for what their bungles do, and unlike our shared gentleman ancestors, Harry will find a way to take such people out. That's what they don't yet understand in Big Loft and across the county on this. He and I think a big, big bungle is being planned – *intentionally* – for the *Lofton County Free Voice.* We've got maybe three days to figure it all out."

"Unit 6, together again," Mrs. Hamilton said nervously.

"We are peace officers now," Captain Hamilton said, "but some folks may have to find out that if they don't want it peaceful, they can be thoroughly obliged."

Chapter 7: Two Meetings

Captain Hamilton had correctly predicted the disposition of the *Lofton County Free Voice:* its principals were smart enough not to have a central location to put out the paper. Its editorial staff met by conference call most often, talking informally as they ran across each other on their regular and known routines.

Printing was done quietly, at printers some of the staff regularly went to for work projects – a quick turn to the side, a flash drive plugged into a printer, being paid for at the printer's card reader with a card preloaded with cash at a kiosk, and copies of the *Lofton County Free Voice* quietly and efficiently were printed by the printer while those responsible for getting it printed went about their regular routines. The card and flash drive were removed – and all record of what had been done went with that removal as the printer rebooted for the next customer.

On to the designated place for the next step: a casual meeting at someone's home for food, fun, fellowship, and folding: the 11X17 sheets had to be carefully folded in quarters so there would be no chance of them getting crumpled or rippled because of their size, and so they would fit easily into the work bags of those who would post them, either before going to graveyard shift jobs or before going to day shift work on the commute to Big Loft or Roanoke. Big carpools, shared gas costs subsidized by the paper, and a team of people assigned to a segment of the towns and county, who could post up their assigned area and get on to the next ones and then to work with such speed that they would not be easily detected and identified.

By the time the papers were posted on the very first day, the reporters – some of them trained journalists, some of them younger interns enjoying on-the-job training fanned out to record the results. That spread of reporters would only happen that one time, and they had netted a bunch of fine reactions from people the *Lofton County Free Voice* would be digging into for weeks, months, and years. A lot of its reporting was not field reporting, because of the potential risk to those known to be identified with the paper. Instead, people quietly researching, along with record pulls and requests both big and small, and then phone calls to relevant officials, made up much of its content. The conference calls were where things were pulled together.

Still, from time to time, a face-to-face meeting was necessary between principals. Lofton County's sudden and complete capitulation to the *Lofton County Free Voice's* Freedom of Information Act requests was such an occasion.

Although James Varick IV had his name as editor-in-chief on the first edition of the *Lofton County Free Voice,* nobody in Lofton County who did not know for sure had quite connected the dots. Few people even in the Black community knew that the community gospel choir leader had such an interesting second life – he was best known for his musicianship, and his ability to get just about anyone to sound good together. The hundreds of children who had gone in and out of his children's choirs knew him as "Uncle Jim." That friendly, harmless moniker had stuck; the gentle giant of music was accounted by no one as a personal threat.

Still less was Mr. Harvey Harrison, who had announced himself as "Marcus Garvey" for a publisher name, accounted as a threat – he was a pleasant middle-aged gentleman not known for publishing anything more controversial than the newsletter for the Smallwood Community Center.

Mr. Thomas Stepforth Sr. was known to be increasingly active in Tinyville's Black community with its youth, but no one had dreamed of his role with the paper – chief financier. He was the wealthiest man in Tinyville, bar none, and would give the richest Loftons of Lofton County serious pause about their wealth superiority had he been so unwise as to flaunt his wealth. He was not. He dressed quietly and lived quietly, and kept a firm grip on his grandchildren and their friends in his daily life... and quietly directed $1 million to a blind trust he had set up for the *Lofton County Free Voice,* with Mr. Varick and Mr. Harrison as trustees with him. He had grown up in Lofton County, and shared with them a deep passion for a righting of the injustice Black people had suffered and continued to suffer. It was a joy to him to share his resources and his technical expertise with them in running a decentralized physical newspaper.

However, the *Lofton County Free Voice* now faced its first serious physical challenge, requiring a rare meeting ... but Mr. Stepforth was known to pack up his Baby Steps – his three youngest grandchildren – and head out to places like the Smallwood Community Center every day of the week. Mr. Varick's choirs routinely made the rounds of Lofton County's community centers, so it was also not out of the ordinary for him to be in the Smallwood Community Center – and, in fact, his children's choir was scheduled to perform at an event the next week. So, it raised no eyebrows anywhere when Mr. Varick and Mr. Stepforth arrived in Mr. Harrison's workplace.

Mr. Stepforth had arrived in time to let his little ones join the Little Steppers dance class for preschool through first grade, and while he watched them, Mr. Varick settled down beside him on one side, and Mr. Harrison, on his break, settled on the other. Just three Black men of mature age, watching over the children – in more ways than one.

"Who would have thought the county would have just given in like that?" Mr. Harrison said.

"Shocking, and suspicious," Mr. Stepforth said.

"Indeed," Mr. Varick said. "They are trying to drown us in data. Tinyville generated five thick folders; Big Loft alone will have 30 to 40 times that amount of data, and then the county will have twice as much as that. Tinyville's police department was big for the size of the town, but lazy; there are indeed 48 cases that need to be reopened, but there is mostly a pattern of harassment and false arrests that lead to no further legal ramifications. Most of the time, the folks in Tinyville couldn't be bothered to follow through."

"Captain Sidney was 78," Mr. Harrison said. "By the end, messing with us was just a pastime – the 48 happen all at the beginning of the ten years we asked for. His house was already paid off, after all."

"Indeed, but we are digressing," Mr. Stepforth said. "Assume five thick folders for each of the small towns, 150 for Big Loft, and 300 for the county, and we have 475 folders to pick up from five different locations, and that much data to crunch."

"We aren't going to be able to get that done before the next paper comes out – it will have to suffice us to announce this week that Lofton County has surrendered and turned over the data," Mr. Varick said. "Captain Hamilton's suggestion about dripping content will have to be taken as well; there is no way to get that much information out in any one or even 20 issues."

"The key thing is to sort out what is important to go first," Mr. Harrison said. "Captain Hamilton's sorting and indexing will be helpful to us in looking at the whole mess we are about to be handed tomorrow. We can use his sort to do our sorts, but we must decide what to present to our readers first. Is it the convictions that have been unjustly obtained, the pattern of false arrests and harassment, the officers who are the absolute worst?"

"My thought is that the pattern of harassment and false arrest sets the tone to discuss the more egregious matters – but until we know what we are getting, I can't say that for sure," said Mr. Varick. "Let me solve the first issue, though: I'll go pick up the data, after we get the paper out

Friday. No one else needs to be tagged with this. We need to pull or so 12 people together to receive the information, but there is no need for them to be identified."

"Wait a moment," Mr. Stepforth said. "The odds on you being tailed are very high, Jim. Previous to this, the paper has *never* had its representatives in one central place, working."

"Good point," Mr. Harrison said. "You do have to take all that stuff somewhere, Jim, and that does require a location."

Mr. Varick considered this, and then slowly shook his head.

"Ah, so *that's* why..."

"I can think of several workarounds," Mr. Stepforth said, "but you know, I guarantee you that the people in question do not think we are intelligent enough to think out workarounds. What if we let them believe what they want to believe, and see what happens?"

Mr. Varick and Mr. Harrison thought about that for a long moment.

"Big risk," Mr. Harrison said. "Potentially big reward. Great story that may well be our way in to sharing the rest of this data."

"I like it," said Mr. Varick. "I know of three buildings we can use to do the sort you have in mind, Thomas."

"One of them is in Tinyville," Mr. Stepforth said. "Let's use that one

– and we'll see how interested the captain there truly is in law and justice."

Mr. Varick smiled thinly.

"He is somewhat interested in the concepts, as far as he understands them. I would say that he is learning."

"That's something, in these parts," Mr. Harrison said. "Can either of you feel him out by tomorrow?"

"I'll do it," Mr. Stepforth said. "Your assessment fits with mine, Jim – he is open to learning, and he is at least approachable. We don't need him, but I'll find out if we can get his help."

Privately, because Mr. Stepforth knew Captain Hamilton's record as an investigator, Mr. Stepforth thought that it was possible that the captain might already be thinking on a similar line as he and Mr. Varick and Mr. Harrison. Yet it was still necessary to proceed with great caution. The risk was immense, and gaining the reward would be costly in many ways. Captain Hamilton's interest in justice might not be quite that large – or at least, he might not see the needs of 28 percent of Tinyville as equivalent to the cost. Still, it was worth carefully making the attempt.

Captain Hamilton at that moment was in fact thinking of the *Lofton County Free Voice* and its constituents, quietly enjoying the sad irony of the need for their existence while an example of the need was yelling in his face.

Mrs. Mary Leigh had come all the way to the police station because a window had been broken out again – not at her house, but at the Gilligan House, once a stately mansion in the days of the antebellum South, now a somewhat neglected landmark of a town and county that did not want it – or shall we say, goodly portions of 72 percent of the town and 61 percent of the county did not want it.

However, the Gilligan House had been a spot on the Underground Railroad, once the only one, then the first in anything closing in on a major city after what was now Fruitland Memorial Park had been freed by its new owner, General J.J. Lofton, in 1839. General Lofton's attitude toward slavery, even through his final years as a Confederate, was that it was antiquated evil that needed to be dispatched willingly (but not by external force, which is why he had died just after the battle of Cold Harbor, in the field, which act had made inevitable the combined 80 miles he and his brother had owned becoming Lofton County. Virginia could not resist making yet another idol out of someone who didn't want that).

Mr. Gilligan, contemporaneous with the general in the 1840s, did not share the general's opinion, but his slaves built him a house with extra rooms anyway, and ran the Railroad right through his house for 20 years! Thus, it had actually been Mr. Varick and Mr. Harrison, with the help of friends, who had gone through all the processes to make the building a county landmark, and then a state landmark. It could therefore not be demolished.

Lofton County's powers-that-be were furious at being outwitted and end-run by the future founders of the *Lofton County Free Voice* – so, the decision was made to destroy the Gilligan House by attrition, through neglect. It was working, although since the building was open to the public and county wasn't paying attention, it was working very, very slowly – people came and worked on the interior regularly, essentially donating labor, time, and materials to the Gilligan House, to keep it as long as possible.

Mr. Varick and Mr. Harrison had not neglected to mention the Gilligan House and official indifference to it in the very first edition of the *Lofton County Free Voice*: they rubbed it in the county's face by putting forth the history of what the building had been and why it was important to Lofton County having a true understanding of itself. Yet they knew that it was a losing battle, in the end. No one had wanted to put the money together to save the building by buying and renovating it outright (Mr. Thomas Stepforth Sr. had not returned to the county yet). Their choosing to put it forth as a landmark was a last resort to preserve it for just one more generation.

That generation's children was just playing catch on the yard, since there was no security, and the ball had gone through a window of the house. Not even a police matter, really. But, Mary Leigh wanted done what she and others wanted done.

"This wouldn't have even happened if that building were just taken down and something useful put in its place!" she said.

Captain Hamilton retained his usual calm, with an effort.

"It is a landmark, which means it is useful in its historical value," he said.

"Oh, nonsense – it has no value to anyone whose history is important!"

"I would venture to say 28 percent of Tinyville and 39 percent of Lofton County would disagree with that opinion."

"I am so tired of these Negroes having to be considered in every decision made in this county – I tell you, it is ridiculous! Their endless demands for recognition!"

"It does tend to be that, among free people, the wishes of three or four out of every ten should be at least considered."

"You're a panty-waist verging on being a traitor to the Southern cause, Captain!"

"The cause was defeated 154 years ago, so I can't say I'm terribly worried about that. What I am concerned about is maintaining peace and justice for all law-abiding citizens of Tinyville – and that citizenship question has also been settled for 150 years. That is the law. As a law enforcement officer, I have no authority to do or say anything that would question the reality of full Black inclusion in the civil process in Tinyville, Lofton County, Virginia, or the United States of America."

Lieutenant O'Reilly watched in amazement at how his captain shook off the insults of his irate old interlocutor with easy calm, a calm that only provoked Mrs. Leigh.

"You were born in Tinyville – out of the best of Virginia's mingled stock! How did you get so weak?"

"Must be the fact that I am a great-great-great grandchild of the one man in Virginia who knew it was over when it was over, and who seems to have carried the knowledge with him to his vault in Lexington, in a sad October of 1870."

Lieutenant O'Reilly suddenly saw just a little of that all-too-familiar face in Virginia's history, in his captain's profile...

Mrs. Leigh could not do anything with what Captain Hamilton had said; she stuttered and stammered and then stopped, in complete confusion.

"I've already investigated the broken window, Mrs. Leigh. We're not going to charge a whole bunch of little kids looking for a place to play in the summer for trespassing when they had no way of knowing they were trespassing, and we're not going to jack their parents up, either. County has needed to put up a fence and properly care for the landmark for 20 years; the responsibility for neglect and all the resulting problems is on the county. That ends this department's involvement in the matter. I hope that is clear now, Mrs. Leigh."

"You mean you intend to let this travesty continue?"

"I have no authority to do anything more than what has been done."

"Useless to all greater purposes – you're useless!"

"Then I suppose you are wasting your valuable time, ma'am, in continuing this conversation."

Mrs. Leigh sputtered to a halt again, and Lieutenant O'Reilly stifled his laughter by getting up and opening the door for the angry woman as she stomped out.

"Wait," Captain Hamilton said as Mrs. Leigh's footsteps went out of hearing, "and, now, Lieutenant."

Lieutenant O'Reilly put his head on his desk and laughed until he cried.

"I don't know how you do it, Captain!" he said. "You never frowned or raised your voice or cussed her out – I know I would have cussed her out, because there are no weak people who can do what we do every day!"

Captain Hamilton smiled at last.

"Indeed there are not," he said. "I'll tell you the secret, and it will be of great use to you as a young Christian at the age of 25: settle in your mind now that as a White man you are walking the earth as a man and are not and at no time will seek the privileges of being treated as a god, but will walk with God and do no more and no less than what He commands."

"That's deep," said Lieutenant O'Reilly. "I mean, I sort of know that, but think about what that does to our thinking about the Southern past and the nation's future. What if every church had taught us that, 400 years ago?"

"The past cannot be changed," Captain Hamilton said. "It is for you today, and tomorrow, and the rest of your life, to consider it. The slave owner was a worse-case scenario in terms of indulging delusions to godhood, but that same delusion would have caused me to be very unkind to Mrs. Leigh. It would cause me to mistreat you, my family, and this town, daily.

"Yet if I am but a man, lower than the angels, finite, limited, and mortal like everyone else around me, how am I justified in pretending to be above anyone else? And, if I am a Christian, following a Savior Who was servant to all, and who submitted Himself to the insults of man while He was God in order that the Father's will be carried out, who am I not to serve and submit, so that the Father's will may be done?"

"That's deep," Lieutenant O'Reilly said, "yet I know the Scripture says the servant is not greater than his master, but can be like him – so, you're right. Either God can be God or we can try at it – not both."

"Right," said Captain Hamilton. "Get that through your mind and your spirit now, because Mrs. Leigh or someone like her might come back in here, and I'll need you to remind me. Don't think I'm perfect. I wanted to slap her with the hand of ten thousand angels, as one my favorite YouTube comediennes, Ms. Shirleen, said, but she also said,

'That ain't of Him — that ain't what He wants.' ”

Lieutenant O'Reilly fell over onto his desk again.

“I saw that one!” he said between laughs. “I guess we're in the law bedazzling business!”

“You're actually right,” Captain Hamilton said. “The Scripture says our lives are to adorn the doctrine we believe, and since our livelihood is as law men, you're right. We adorn the doctrine with how we go about fairly and justly upholding the law.”

Lieutenant O'Reilly froze.

“Captain, do you realize that since what you are saying is true, that means that the entire so-called history of so-called Christian America is questionab--.”

“Lieutenant, we don't even have time to deal with that today. You're right, but we don't even have time to deal with it properly. We've got to go house hunting.”

“What?”

“It's a police matter, about to happen. When the *Lofton County Free Voice* picks up all that material from the departments next to ours, it is about to go down like it is 1869 in Lofton County. If I knew how and when, we could stop it today, but, I don't, so we are going to go get evidence together so we are ready. Turn on the phone forwarding service to my cell; we're both going out on a call for house-hunting, because I want you to understand should something happen to me what the motives are, and how the evidence connects."

"Please don't get hurt, Captain," said Lieutenant O'Reilly. "I'm not ready to be acting captain."

"The first step is knowing that," Captain Hamilton said. "The next step is to be willing to learn, and to get ready. I'm not trying to leave you, but, just in case, let's have you ready to handle what's coming."

Captain Hamilton paused, and then his face turned grim.

"We may be grateful for Mrs. Leigh in the end," he said. "She provided both a good reminder of what is at stake, and from what direction it may come, and even who encourages the kinds of things we are likely to face. You'll see what I am talking about in a little while. Let's go."

Chapter 8: House-Hunting and Shopping for Clues

Mrs. Hamilton was pleasantly surprised to see her husband's pickup truck pull up in the front yard in the middle of the day.

"Adella! Agnes! Iris! Get some snacks together for your dad and his lieutenant!"

Lieutenant O'Reilly knew everyone in the family already. "Hey, Brother Pat!" Addison yelled across the house, thereby leading to him being gently reprimanded for yelling across the house. Brother Pat was glad for the refreshments and to sit for several minutes with the captain's eldest daughter, Adella, who had inherited her mother's auburn hair, warm amber eyes, and generous figure, with her father's marble coloring and tautness of frame.

Not that Lieutenant O'Reilly even thought about asking Miss Hamilton out. To him, that would have been like asking a daughter of General Robert E. Lee out – and no one had ever been successful in the end in doing that, history shows. It was just nice to be allowed to sit in Miss Hamilton's presence for several minutes, owing to her father's generosity to his other children: his four youngest children had jumped on him and were asking him to stay and play.

"I'm still on duty, sweethearts, but that includes duty to you... ."

Thus he spent ten minutes playing with his children before coming to show the lieutenant the house and to say what he had wanted to say.

"Take this as a baseline, Lieutenant, for what we are about to see. I bought this overgrown farmhouse at a short sale – that is, the owners wanted to get out from under it for just enough to pay off the mortgage. I was able to do one better than that; the couple was happy to take over my apartment lease in Big Loft, so they had their new place to stay and I had somewhere to bring my family! But it would still take $20,000 more to get the whole house presentable to my 12!

"This farmhouse, the land it sits on, and the renovations are worth a total of $110,000 – short sale plus renovations. Compare that to my family's yearly take-home income through last year: $210,000 yearly. Obviously, a lot of that comes from investments, Reserve checks, and Ham It Up; my Tinyville check was not even cut when the Lord brought me to this house. Yet bear in mind: with $210,000 to work with per year, this house still represents more than 50 percent of our total income per year.

"Now everybody has not been blessed with 11 children; a couple with just a few children making $210,000 could have taken this on more easily, but then again, if they had any sense, they wouldn't be bothered because of the cost of upkeep on a house this old and this large. On the other hand, how many couples who live and work in Lofton County have a combined income of $210,000?"

"Not many," said Lieutenant O'Reilly. "Very few people own businesses that get beyond the local niche, and still fewer people that have that kind of money are working at all."

"Right. Certainly those aren't law enforcement wages around here. You're a freshly minted lieutenant, just out of the academy. You're pulling $17,500. Tinyville had to do a little better to convince me to move from JAG to police captain; I'm pulling $36,500. If Mrs. Hamilton were making the same, we couldn't do this, not even if we only had two or three children.

"Captain Lee is in Big Loft. They really had to work hard to convince him to come home, and they have more to work with. He's pulling $48,500. If he were married to a wife making what he was, this house would still hurt the Lees badly, and so would anything else in the $100,000 price range. Keep this in mind as we hit the road to see how our other colleagues live."

Once back in the car, Captain Hamilton pulled a big folder from under his seat, and handed it to Lieutenant O'Reilly, who scanned it.

"That's a lot of real estate and business data – when did you have time to do all that, sir?"

"I didn't. That was Captain Lee's doing. He is a meticulous and incurable overachiever unless God mellow him out in later years. You tell me to go find you a good car, I will find you an excellent car and wave at you as you drive off. Captain Lee would get you offers on 10 excellent cars, apologize for not having time to find 15, and then compensate by including his analysis on which one has the most gas mileage, the most durability, the best warranty – and of course none of them would vary more than 1-2 percent either way, but by the time he finished with you, you would know the percentages down to the thousandth place."

"Remind me not to ever do that," Lieutenant O'Reilly said. "We're going to see three houses, just from this, aren't we?"

"You're catching on, Lieutenant. Yet you will be glad for the detail, and how Captain Lee has arranged it, because in just a little while, what is about to happen in Lofton County, and why, will be much clearer to you."

Captain Hamilton looked both ways and then did what people did

123

with four-wheel drive in Lofton County – he headed off the main roads into the informal country road network. Thus a country ride, bumpy and rough, to end up pulling through a field and then onto a more serviced road with a view to the backside of a large mansion that resembled a more modern take on the antebellum plantation houses in their heyday.

"How much is that worth?" Captain Hamilton said, and Lieutenant O'Reilly checked the data.

"Wow. $480,000," he said. "Kind of new for a Lofton manse, though, and not in the right place in the county."

"It's not a Lofton manse; when they do buy something new, they buy in cash," Captain Hamilton said. "Look at the type of mortgage on that thing."

"Oh, no, a Lofton or Slocum or Slocum-Lofton would never get into a mess like this. Their credit is too good even if they didn't buy in cash. Whoever is in there is on borrowed time."

"Look at the salary line for the people who own it," Captain Hamilton said. "Look at the businesses and investments they own – or do they own any?"

"Okay … wait, what?" Lieutenant O'Reilly said.

"Read it all again until you understand the problem," Captain

Hamilton said. "Captain Lee is as accurate as he is meticulous; if his data shows the numbers don't add up, you may be sure they don't add up."

"But, sir, there's no way – you can't get a $480,000 house on a combined $75,000 before-tax income, especially not if you have five children! There's no way!"

"There's no *legal* way," Captain Hamilton said. "Either the mortgage companies have gone back to their old tricks, or the couple in question has some extra-legal sources. Keep reading. You'll find out which."

Lieutenant O'Reilly kept reading.

"The mortgage company is either lying or thinks the couple is bringing in twice what they are bringing in."

"Okay, but, how long has this couple been able to make those payments?"

"Let's see – they haven't missed a payment in the life of the mortgage, which means they do have the money – but how?"

"Now that is the question, Lieutenant. Have a look now at the next page."

"Okay, wait, whaaaaaaaaaaaaaaaaaaaaaaaaaaaaaaaaat?"

"Yep. That's a local police captain and his wife, and that captain is making at least twice as much as Captain Lee, in a town a twentieth the size of Big Loft. How is that?"

Lieutenant O'Reilly shook his head.

"I don't know, sir. Inheritance?"

"Check it out. The information is there."

"Okay … no. No inheritance."

"Bear in mind: he, like me, is captain, chief, and commissioner. His salary and benefits reflect his seven years in the position."

"That's still nowhere near enough."

"Not *legally,* Lieutenant. Remember all that we read on Friday, at 6:30 in the morning, walking through Tinyville?"

Lieutenant O'Reilly jumped so high he would have hit his head on the roof of the cab of the truck had not Captain Hamilton put a hand on his shoulder to hold him down a little.

"Oh, no, sir – oh, no!"

"Hold your horses, Lieutenant. That's not even the worst case," Captain Hamilton said. "Marinate on all of that, and go to the green colored divider page, two thirds of the way to the back of the folder. We're skipping the second case because it is similar to this, but, just understand; as Captain Lee once said, there's no bottom to it."

Lieutenant O'Reilly had been impressed by the $480,000 take on a plantation house with modern touches. He was overwhelmed by the super-sized McMansion – gaudy blue and gold, at least twenty bedrooms on a single level, swimming pool almost Olympic-sized – that Captain Hamilton pulled his truck out of the woods to see, just from the edge of the property.

"Oh, no – no, no, no, no, no, no, no, no, no, no, no, no, no!"

"That was more or less my reaction when I read through the thing this morning too," Captain Hamilton said. "That thing is the most bombastic use of a million-dollar mortgage I have ever seen, purchased by a man with no known investments, no known businesses, officially making $42,000 a year. Wife makes $35,000, no known investments, no known businesses. Go to the last page, look at the name, and you'll *truly* understand Friday."

Lieutenant O'Reilly looked, closed the folder, and put his head in his hands.

"Oh, no. No, no, no, no, no."

"Remember, Lieutenant: racism is never just about looking down on people different from us because of ethnic characteristics. Racism is about *profit, always*. There is a good reason that the *Lofton County Free*

Voice asked for exactly ten years of data, and you're looking at the worst of 25 reasons.

"Not everyone is this open about it – some people are smart enough to plow their ill-gotten gains into things that people can't see driving around the county. Yet the fact that there are 25 cases that everyone can see means that the anger of the *Free Voice* is understandable. Anyone who can see knows the people that own these 25 residences are not bringing home the median wage for the county – and yet they are working in law enforcement, and somehow pulling that kind of money out while innocent people –."

"I will never – Lord God, I will never complain about my honestly made $17,500 again. I will never complain about any honestly made money again – oh, God, forgive me, keep me off the first step down the path that leads to this! Oh, God, keep me!" Lieutenant O'Reilly said.

"The fact that you realize that at 25," Captain Hamilton said, "means that the Lord is already doing what you have asked of Him. Now, when you see the rest of what I have at the office, it will make perfect sense to you."

The captain and his lieutenant could not go right back to the office, as a county call involving the end of a rash of home invasions came out.

Since there were dead bodies, Captain Hamilton got the call. After officially determining that the would-be home invaders had died in the commission of their crime, Captain Hamilton and Lieutenant O'Reilly returned to the office to do their reports and review more data related to what they had been on the road seeing.

"I know I look and feel like Captain Lee now," Lieutenant O'Reilly said glumly, at the end.

"Just a little," Captain Hamilton said. "Yet I find joy in knowing that God has us here to do some good. I try to keep my eyes fixed on that, Lieutenant. It is a privilege to be alive in troubled times, to do right."

The phone rang.

"Hello?" said Captain Hamilton. "Good afternoon, Mr. Stepforth. Yes … Friday? Really? They are all giving in? Well, that's good, isn't it? … No? … The Gilligan House for the weekend … Well, it's a public building, so plenty of transparency … actually, I had thought about that too … it's a possibility … you just need backup … that's good because we are a two-man department … well, thank you, sir, we do emphasize brains over brawn, but you had better find some brawn, because in all of the county I can only think of one other officer for sure that I could trust

... look, Mr. Stepforth, Captain Lee no more chose his name or face than you chose your color, so I expect you and yours to check your prejudices like I have to check mine ... he has uncovered information that will allow us both to exonerate many of the innocent and grab hold of the guilty, perhaps in one weekend, of his own accord ... content of character, as Dr. King taught us ... .

"All right ... well, I can do that much ... I'll set up a free conference call for us since I can understand, with all that has happened, why y'all don't want an official law enforcement officer to know your conference call number ... I'll call you back in 20 minutes with some times and a number ... the pickup is Friday afternoon? ... okay, we should talk no later than tomorrow night ... yes, after prayer meeting, because we all are going to need to get prayed up for real ... all right. I'll call you back. Goodbye."

Captain Hamilton got off the phone and shook his head.

"Working Wednesday night?"

"No – free for whatever we need to do," Lieutenant O'Reilly said.

"Excellent. Let me call –."

The phone rang.

"Hello? Captain Lee, how did you know I was thinking of talking with you? Hold on a moment so Lieutenant O'Reilly can hear you."

Captain Hamilton put the phone on speaker, and the soft but full tenor of Captain Lee filled the office, in all its grim gravity.

"I thought that you should know this detail – I am in the parking lot here at Big Discounts For Your Loft, the largest purveyor of household furnishings in the county, including bedroom sets and furnishings. I was told by the desk clerk that I was at least the 15th officer he had seen coming in since yesterday. I asked what my counterparts were finding so interesting."

Captain Hamilton put his head on his hand and started laughing.

"Oh, no, Captain Lee, no! No, they didn't!"

"Of course they did, Captain Hamilton. You know that no one has had a new idea for 150 years – or 400, depending on who you ask."

"I don't get it," Lieutenant O'Reilly said.

"Your captain has an ability to laugh in order to keep from crying that I wish I possessed," Captain Lee said. "At the time of his choosing, he will apprise you of the causes of his reaction."

"I'm all right now, Captain Lee," Captain Hamilton said. "I just had to do that or just have a real fit. Continue your statement."

"I am still sitting in the lot, and three more of our colleagues have gone in. I have photographs of them, and have in hand a list of the previous purchases – 17 men, mostly from county and Big Loft. I will send you the complete list when I have it."

"How did you get a warrant for all that so soon?"

"I didn't need it. No crime has yet been committed except against good sense, and as for the rest, the genetic advantage I have in returning to Virginia is that generally speaking, I can get what I want with a smile, especially if the person I am speaking with is a pretty young Southern belle who grew up unfortunately idolizing my face in stone."

"Oh, you know, that smile in Virginia could open just about every door and vault there is. I'll be looking for your scan. Meanwhile, I have just been in contact with the folks from the *Lofton County Free Voice,* and they are on the same line that we are. Are you available for a conference call on Wednesday night, let's say at eight?"

"Yes, Captain, I am."

"I'll send you the number in 15 minutes."

"Very well."

Captain Hamilton hung up the phone and turned to his computer, and put in ten minutes getting the conference call line set up. Then he called Mr. Stepforth back.

"I'm sending you the conference call number and the code by text, but I wanted to tell you that the possibility we discussed based on history is rapidly becoming a high probability based on actual events. There is a run on bedroom furnishings at Big Discounts for Your Loft --."

Lieutenant O'Reilly heard Mr. Stepforth break out laughing and shout – "Oh, no, Captain, no – they are not that backwards!"

"It appears that they might well be," Captain Hamilton said. "I'll have full evidence about it in hand by tonight. Meanwhile, expect the conference call info imminently … right … right … I'll check in with you tomorrow afternoon."

Captain Hamilton hung up the phone, and spent several moments texting. The phone rung again –.

"Confirming receipt," Captain Lee said, "and the call has been calendared. I will report to you tonight with the rest of the information."

"Very good; I'll speak with you later."

Captain Hamilton hung up the phone and sighed.

"I still don't get it," Lieutenant O'Reilly said.

"Regular domestic terrorists keep their uniforms and outfits ready, but even weekend race warriors want a nice crisp appearance in their white, so of course they didn't take their old pillowcases and bedsheets off their beds to use."

Lieutenant O'Reilly thought about that for a moment, and then jumped.

"*That's* what they were buying at – oh, no, no, no, no, no, no!"

Lieutenant O'Reilly jumped up, his hands to his head, and began pacing the room.

"It's 2019 – when are they going to at least modernize their racism?"

"Hang on to outmoded lies, and this is how you end up – for real. Meanwhile, Lieutenant, I told you when we met that if you haven't done your will, you need to. Today is Tuesday. You have only three days to get it done."

Chapter 9: The Angel of Death Is Awakened

Tuesday evening: on his way out of Big Loft's police headquarters, Captain Lee heard someone calling his name. He turned around and looked down the street -- .

"Commissioner Thomas, good evening."

"Good evening, Captain Lee! I'm glad I was able to catch up with you – that traffic out there is horrible! Can I buy you a drink?"

"I don't drink, Commissioner, but I will enjoy a virgin *mojito* in your company if you desire."

So: down the street and around the corner to the Blue Line Bar, a favorite of police big wigs in Big Loft. Commissioner Thomas looked on with great intrigue as Captain Lee had his virgin *mojito* – three limes, a whole bunch of mint, molasses, cool water – made to order while the commissioner enjoyed a big mug of his favorite draft beer.

"I just wanted to get out of the shop for a minute to talk shop, but, you know how it is," said Commissioner Thomas.

"Yes, sir."

"First let me say again, thank you, Captain Lee, for coming out of the army to help your hometown in its time of need – I don't know how we would be able to handle this whole Freedom of Information Act thing without you working on it."

"Thank you, sir."

"You do have it ready for release on Friday, yes?"

"It will be on your desk for review in the morning. Had I known that you would be back at headquarters this evening I would have presented it to you before we left."

"Oh, no, I didn't expect to be back tonight and there was no need for that. I am going to just have a look at your summary; nobody else has time to go through almost 200 folders of data. I feel sorry for that paper, that they have to go through it."

Captain Lee registered that the commissioner had told his first outright lie of the evening. At such close proximity, no one without special training could control their body language well enough to fool the colonel from Special Forces.

"It was such a blessing that you brought fresh eyes to the thing, just a blessing," the commissioner continued. "People in the middle of it tend to get bogged down in the details they were involved in, but it is so good that you don't know anything and could see the broad picture."

The beer had gone to the commissioner's head a little too soon. Of course, Captain Lee already knew he had been brought in as a dupe, and handed a task that he was supposed to rush through in order to save more time to work his cold cases. Nonetheless, the fact that the commissioner had said it to his face infuriated him. That was what the big mint limeade was for, and he kept sipping it in a measured way to control his heart rate, blood pressure, and temper.

On the other hand, when the enemy was dumb enough to reveal his position … .

"My summary does contain a broad overview," Captain Lee said, "and it will be ready for you in the morning."

"Good, Captain. That's what I wanted to know. I hear nothing but accolades coming to you from every corner of the department –."

A second and immense lie!

" – and our getting through this crisis will seal up the sum."

"No doubt it will, Commissioner."

The conversation turned away from shop, at least on the commissioner's side; he relaxed and talked more and did not notice that Captain Lee had nothing else of substance to say, but merely made listening noises, his dark eyes focusing on the progress of the life-saving elixir downward in his glass as he swallowed it at the necessary intervals.

At an appropriate time – because the commissioner was going to stay and drink quite a bit more – the captain excused himself, walked back around the corner and up the street, and returned to his office. He opened up the first of the file folders to be turned over on Friday and took off the summary that was there. He then started up his computer and typed up the kind of broad overview the commissioner wanted to see, leaving the first summary for inclusion in the files he would hand over to the *Lofton County Free Voice.*

Captain Lee then left for the night and went to his studio apartment, looked through his large music collection, put on Jobim, went to his refrigerator, and pulled out the dinner he had made for himself in the morning – curry spinach and hard boiled eggs – and an indulgent dessert: a whole hunk of ginger, steeped in lemon juice and honey. Thus passed away the first part of his night, and he settled into sleep in his armchair.

Captain Lee woke up three hours later and found himself going from pleasantly waking, in the exactly eight seconds it took for his clear mind to assemble certain facts from Saturday to that day, to completely enraged. His blood pressure went through a corresponding spike, but it had been low while he was sleeping owing to his having taken his medicine while eating, so, there was some room for his pressure to rise and fall safely.

If that had been the only problem, but no … he had been triggered. His mind had gone into an entirely different gear. Colonel Lee now looked out of the dark eyes of the police captain ... Colonel Lee in that first year after Five Bright Nine, Colonel Lee outraged by the callous indifference of his superiors to the needless deaths of his men, Colonel Lee who at such times had all too much in common with his equally deadly ancestral uncle, of the same rank when he made the decision to join the Rebellion.

There was an important difference between the Colonels Lee, however: one had begun as an military engineer. The other had begun in Special Forces. That is to say, the modern Lee had much more knowledge of ways and means to do folks in, so much so that he had earned a nickname in the army: the Angel of Death. He was on a desk job at the police force for a reason, having not wanted to be in any situation that triggered that portion of him, but, the situation had found him.

**

Captain Hamilton and his family were completing dinner by the time Captain Lee got home, and soon after that, Captain Hamilton was on his home computer, communicating in writing with Ham It Up's suppliers about the month's invoices and requisitions. On screenshare and a conference call line was Ironwood Hamilton Jr., the captain's firstborn, who was also working that aspect of the business, and whom the captain had prepared to take it over entirely should anything happen to him. This sort of training had been going on for years, but Ironwood Jr. noted his father's seriousness that particular evening.

"Things going bad already in Tinyville, Dad?"

"Yes, son, they are. Friday night, Saturday morning – likely to get kind of rough."

"Dad, if it comes to it, I've got this down. But I'll be praying that you'll be back to take it up again."

"So am I, son. This is where we have to trust God."

"Yes, Dad, I know. How's Mom holding up?"

"Trusting God, son, and praying."

"What about you?"

"See previous answer."

"All right, Dad, I get it."

"I'm not happy, son, about this thing. But I knew there was trouble when I came, and I don't think my work is done here. If it's not, I'll talk with you Saturday night."

"I'll be praying for and looking forward to it."

Ironwood Jr. had another thought.

"How is Cousin Harry?"

"Not too good, son. Getting better overall, but this thing has opened up some doors in him that were better left shut. Pray for your cousin."

"I will, Dad."

"You have it from here?"

"Yes, Dad, go on and be with the crew. Good night."

"Love you, son."

"Love you too, Dad. Be careful out there."

"I will, son. You watch out for yourself in New York City too. Tinyville ain't the only dangerous place in the world, you know."

Ironwood Jr. laughed.

"Always that way with words – good night, Dad."

"Good night, son."

Captain Hamilton shut down his screen, and then went over to check on his wife Agnes, who was on her computer doing wholesale orders.

"How are we doing over here?" he said.

"These stupid tariffs, Woody, these stupid tariffs … my regular suppliers are struggling to be profitable because of it, and they are out of stock more and more often. How do you buy American when America doesn't produce what you need – tariffs don't solve that, and are driving businesses out of business."

"I know, darling," said Captain Hamilton. "Take a break for a few minutes … your shoulders are holding as much tension as mine, and you know we can't have that."

Mrs. Hamilton smiled as her husband wrapped his powerful hands around her shoulders and began a deep massage.

"Oh, that feels so good, Woody... oh that feels so good … I guess I am stressing and I don't need to be … the Lord is our Supply, and always will be … what I'm really stressing about is not moonstones …"

"I know, darling."

"You told me it was not going to be easy being here, but you know I'm from New York and I didn't think Tinyville would offer up this kind of trouble. I was wrong. You were right."

"I ought to give you a massage more often, Aggie."

"I agree. But stop interrupting while I'm confessing."

"Yes, dear. Carry on."

"I didn't believe you 24 years ago when you told me how it was, and I didn't believe you when you said how it would be. At least in New York, or even in Roanoke or Big Loft, at least you wouldn't be by yourself, but this is ridiculous.

"You should have heard Mrs. Mary Leigh at the store, complaining to her friends – Ira and Agnew combined don't whine that much."

The yearling twins, hearing their names, looked up for a moment. Ira squealed … .

"Don't worry about it, Ira," his father said gently.

Ira went right back to his blocks, and Agnew followed his lead.

"Ira is definitely the New Yorker," Captain Hamilton said.

Mrs. Hamilton cracked up laughing, which got her sons' complete attention, to the point that they started laughing, and then their father started laughing because all of them were laughing. He went and got the Baby Hams, and they and their parents enjoyed a nice half-hour playing and laughing. The yearlings got sleepy after that, and their mother let them sleep on her lap as their father took her place at the computer and finished up the wholesale orders.

By the time Captain Hamilton finished the orders, Mrs. Hamilton was asleep with her baby children, and Ilene and Allison had come in and snuggled up with her and gone to sleep as well.   Captain

Hamilton kissed every face tenderly, and then left the room before his

emotions overcame him. Later, when he and Mrs. Hamilton finally had

the bed to themselves, she could feel both his deep exhaustion but also

the deep emotion in the captain's good night kiss … and also the faint

stirring of arousal within him, competing with his need to sleep.

"Sweet dreams, Woody," she teased.

"Oh, they will be," he murmured. "Meet me there …"

"I'll be there, Woody."

***

Wednesday, day: Quiet as usual in Captain Hamilton's office, where the

most exciting event for the day was another three interviews for the

lieutenants' positions. It was getting to be a bit tiresome: the pay was low

and the captain's requirements quite high, and those two things did not

match for most.

Captain Lee's day was a bit more eventful. Commissioner Thomas

reviewed his second summary, and approved the entire release as it was.

Captain Lee merely slipped his first summary under it in the folders that

were actually going to be released, and began packing the folders into the

cases that James Varick IV would eventually put in a U-Haul truck. He kept an eye on the clock, counting the seconds until lunch time.

In the wake of Five Bright Nine, Captain Lee's mindset had altered, perhaps irreversibly: he remained ferociously devoted to his peers and subordinates everywhere, but the instant a superior gave him an indication that he or she was not to be trusted, that superior became a suspect at best and an enemy at worst – and anybody who looked up Henry Fitzhugh Lee's record could tell you that you didn't want him to consider you an enemy.

The clock struck 12 noon. Captain Lee changed clothes and flipped his hair to a more rakish look to fit the role, and became the 13th busboy at the restaurant where the commissioner and his friends were dining. The place had been hiring for a month; nobody thought to question the new busboy with the perfect face and glorious smile, because he bussed with great efficiency and earned great tips for the pool.

Commissioner Thomas did not recognize the new busboy, although he had sat next to the man and had a drink with him the night before. Captain Lee expected that; the commissioner was just the type of person who didn't see you unless you had on the right insignia, and nobody performing one of the slaves' old roles had it. So, Captain Lee cleaned tables, kept customers delighted, and dropped a surveillance device …

"I tell you, Lee has worked out better than we dreamed. He managed the whole thing but not too well, judging from his summary. Too much data for any one man to completely understand in that short period of time, but he has done a workmanlike job that will cover us in every event."

"Yeah; chances are with that much data, no one will be able to do any better than he did," sad another big wig.

"Let's hope so," said the commissioner. "We have enough problems policing Big Loft without that Negro paper dragging up old skeletons. It's going to be close enough still, the way Lee picks up detail."

"He surely does," said a secretary. "He remembered my birthday and divined my favorite color just from what was on my desk – brought me the most lovely card last week!"

"Oh, don't go getting sweet on him!" the other men at table thundered in unison at the blushing belle beauty.

"It's kind of hard not to," she said defiantly. "He's so handsome, and so sweet in his own, sad way ... and he's not dumb either. It took 24 years to wrap up that Swanson case, didn't it?"

"Lee solved it in a week," said the commissioner. "That's what makes him so wonderful, and so dangerous. That meticulous mind – my fear was that he was going to do so well that he was going to leave a road map for that paper to follow to understand the whole mess."

(Which Captain Lee had, and would.)

"I'm still glad we have Captain Bragg's full plan as backup," said another bigwig.

The commissioner chuckled.

"We can't talk about that, not even unofficially, and not officially until Saturday morning – but you're right, it is good that we have worked things out with Captain Bragg, and that we have folks to work with him all the way."

Unfortunately for the commissioner, by Saturday morning, that statement would become part of the official record, even though he would not be alive to know about that.

James Varick IV was sitting in his car at 1:30pm when his notification bell for the *Free Voice* tip line Facebook page lit up. Most people had missed that little detail in the first issue, but apparently, not everyone; someone had liked and followed the page and dropped a recording – a recording that made Mr. Varick jump when he heard the names of the people referred to, and recognized Commissioner Thomas's voice.

The dropper – Facebook handle "Friend to Freedom" – had left a single note as the entry photo: "Watch this space, LCFV." Below it was a link to the recording, and below that a post: "More information forthcoming."

With trembling hands, Mr. Varick downloaded the recording and then transcribed it on his laptop, then added it to his notes for the evening's conference call just before Mr. Harrison called.

"Jim – do you see what's on the tip page?"

"I've already transcribed it and I'm sending it to you. It's the commissioner and his two deputies and two of their secretaries."

"Jim – we're going to have to run back-to-back issues!"

"Hold on – Nathan is calling in – let's go three-way – ."

"Hello? Harvey and Uncle Jim, do you see what just popped up in the tip line?"

"Should make tonight's conference call even more interesting," Mr. Varick said.

"I'd like to see Hamilton field those questions!"

"It will be as new to him as it is to us," Mr. Varick said. "I'll send you the number, Nathan – call in but don't *butt in*. Am I making myself very clear, Nathan?"

"Yes, Uncle. What time?"

"Eight. After prayer meeting."

"Yeah, I think we are going to need that today – and a whole lot of other people are going to need it that don't even know they need it yet," said Mr. Harrison with a chuckle.

Chapter 10: Those Time-Honored Rituals

Wednesday night: "A council of war in 2019," Captain Lee said darkly to his cousin Captain Hamilton. "Well, those who insist on war surely will have it. It is inevitable."

"I would tell you to calm down," Captain Hamilton said, "but you are calm and nothing could be calmer than death."

"Death passive, or death active?" Captain Lee said without missing a beat.

Captain Hamilton didn't answer that, knowing there was no need to encourage that line of thought in his cousin. Lieutenant O'Reilly's wide green eyes were commentary enough.

The young lieutenant had no idea what had set Captain Lee off, but it was apparent that somebody somewhere had made a mistake, a mistake like rolling along at 22.5 knots through the North Atlantic in a ship named *Titanic*. No one would ever have intentionally run their ship up on an iceberg, had they known it was there. In like manner, no one with a innate sense of self-preservation would ever have triggered Captain Lee, had they just known the danger.

"Here we go," Captain Hamilton said, dialing in the number for the call. Captain Lee sat to the right of him, Lieutenant O'Reilly to the left, which unconsciously mirrored the formation of Mr. Varick, Mr. Harrison, and Mr. Stepforth, with Mr. Turner calling in from his home.

The conference call lasted three productive hours. Captain Hamilton marveled at the spectrum of personalities, with Nathan Turner on the hot end and Harry Lee on the cold, and the perfect balance it produced. The free sharing of information because of the needs of the moment; their discovering together the meaning of what that information meant to crimes past, present, and future, and their working together to create a response that covered all the ground – it was draining, it was terrifying, and it was wonderful.

"I'm so glad I took your advice to get my will done, Captain," Lieutenant O'Reilly said.

"I am too, but, if we do this right, maybe none of us will need to exercise those wills."

Finally, Captain Lee cracked a thin smile.

"At least we won't be outnumbered this time. I like Mr. Turner and I believe he will do a fine job on his part."

"You like him?" Lieutenant O'Reilly said.

"Yes. It has always been about life and death; he has the appropriate emotion for a man whose people have been attacked and harmed. You are not supposed to take it kindly, Lieutenant O'Reilly, if you are a man, and not every man is as even-tempered as your captain. I understand Mr. Turner entirely."

"He would be mortified to know," Captain Hamilton said.

Captain Lee's smile widened.

"I won't tell him, Captain Hamilton. As we have had to grow beyond our prejudices, he must have time to mature as well. We must not play too hard with these younger men."

Lieutenant O'Reilly jumped, and Captain Hamilton got next to him in time to keep him from falling.

"Present company excluded, of course," Captain Lee purred. "You are being properly trained by the right man, Lieutenant O'Reilly. Have no fear at all. If we survive the weekend, you will only be aged by your first taste of real law and order."

As Captain Lee left to begin his drive back to Big Loft, Lieutenant O'Reilly stared at him with a mix of fascination and horror. Captain Hamilton chuckled, a chuckle interrupted by the scream of a child in the street. The two Tinyville police officers ran outside to see a little boy running up the street being chased by an angry flying something. Captain

Lee had turned around, his eyes wide and then narrowing. The little boy passed him – the angry flying something did not, as the Big Loft captain snatched it right out of the sky and then put his hand in a rain barrel in the next instant.

The little boy ran back, astonished.

"What's you do – kill it?" he said.

"No," said Captain Lee. "I slowed her down, but I won't let her die."

And he scooped the half-drowned carpenter bee out of the rain barrel and put her in the sun to dry.

"We only kill when there is no other choice, little man," he said gently. "I could have easily killed her, but it was not necessary for me to do that to help you."

"You're a nice man," the little boy said, and ran up and embraced his rescuer as his mother finally caught up. The mother caught the brilliant warmth of the smile the little boy's sweet affection had surprised in his rescuer, and slowed almost to a stop, dazzled.

"I must be seeing things," Lieutenant O'Reilly said, rubbing his eyes.

"That's Harry Lee for you," Captain Hamilton said softly. "Openly expressing his desire to off some folks in one minute, catching a carpenter bee in the next minute without killing it, could catch a wife and a ready-made family in the next minute, and that's just in one hour. Mr. Turner is more open in his great passionate life, and Captain Lee more reserved and compressed, but they are very similar. Life has also been too vivid and too painful for them to handle easily – unjust deaths, grief, rage, PTSD – similar profiles."

"But what about … that?"

Captain Hamilton shook his head as he turned and went back inside.

"Women and children always know, Lieutenant. Little Byron Berrier doesn't see the marble front; no little child ever has. The widow Berrier saw it in how calmly Captain Lee handled that bee, but, her son having pierced the veil showed her the treasure past the calm mask. If given opportunity, most women in her position would hang on a long time in hopes of gaining such a prize … and it looks like she might have a ghost of a chance because of her secret weapon."

"What?

"Her son."

Sure enough, Captain Lee and the little Berrier family were passing back down the street, the little boy on the captain's broad shoulders enjoying a ride, and the captain and Mrs. Berrier enjoying pleasant conversation.

"Captain Lee loves children," Captain Hamilton said, "and would make as fabulous a stepfather in a case like that as he would a father. My wife is trying to pray him into a second marriage. We'll see what happens to this carpenter bee connection."

By this point, Captain Lee was down the street getting Mrs. Berrier's groceries into the car while she strapped her son into the car seat he was supposed to be in instead of poking a stick into a hole in a telephone pole – a hole that of course had contained a carpenter bee. That little boy still managed to get an arm out a window to wave as his mother drove off, and Captain Lee stood waving back, his glorious full smile still on his face as he turned around to walk back to his car, and thus past the police station window, through which Lieutenant O'Reilly stared with even more fascination and horror.

Captain Hamilton let it ride. After all, they were still looking at Captain Lee's great-great-great-uncle that way, too.

Thursday, day: All around the Gilligan House, the county looked like it had finally come to terms with its Black population, and started hiring its contractors to fix things up. No fence went up, but a whole bunch of digging was going on in the yard – septic tank replacement? – and new grass was brought in and laid over the the spot – just to the side of the front door when done. Inside, the clatter of hammers and the creak of crowbars and the smell of WD-40 were everywhere. The broken window was, notably, *not* replaced.

A group of men came out of the woods onto the back yard of the house, covered in cobwebs but smiling. The significance of this would not be understood until the second issue of the *Lofton County Free Voice* came out on Saturday.

Thursday night: Just after dark, a secretive conference of fighting men met, and an argument about location got heated – and cooled – because of the natures of the two men arguing it:

"Look, man, you're no general over here, and I don't care who your uncle was!"

"I'm not giving orders, just suggestions."

"And you can keep your suggestions to yourself – your family ain't been telling Black people what to do since Arlington finally came into its own as a clearly marked graveyard, and don't you forget that!"

"People are racist. Geometry and bullets aren't. Forget my infamous name, and draw that formation out on paper."

"You draw it, since you're the one that has the problem with it."

"As you wish … your formation, as I understand it."

"That's it."

"Look at what happens if you draw straight lines across the field of potential engagement, here, here, here, and here."

"Well, I'll be … I hadn't accounted for friendly fire. Well, even a stopped clock is right twice a day!"

"Even if the clock's name is Lee, Mr. Turner."

"Well, don't quit with the non-racist geometry now, man. Draw something better with all that West Point education you have."

"As you wish … here is a better formation, and here are the lines of intersection."

"Much better. I see it … I see how the other way would have been a disaster, too."

"Oh, this way here will be a disaster, for the other side if they push it. The idea is to have it be a disaster only for them."

"I like this idea. Your non-racist geometry is welcome any time, although you're still not invited to the cookout."

"What do you mean? I would not miss Friday night for the world."

"Not that cookout."

"After all, you can ask any nephew of Grant how much my family loves a cookout."

"Not that cookout in the Wilderness, or that picnic at Cold Harbor either – you're not supposed to have jokes, Captain Lee."

"I'm not that marble statue, Mr. Turner."

"I see that. Noted."

***

In the Hamilton home, Captain Hamilton completed the last of his semi-public rituals before a serious deployment. Lieutenant O'Reilly and a bunch of his other friends were at the house for "provisions and prayer," and the captain and lieutenant were prayed over by his friends and their families. Captain Lee slipped in toward the end of that, and said a prayer that surprised Lieutenant O'Reilly for its passion and expressiveness. After that, the friends and family had dessert, and then slowly departed to their homes, with Captain Lee and Lieutenant O'Reilly leaving last.

Captain and Mrs. Hamilton eventually put the happily clueless littlest ones – Ilene, Allison, Ira, and Agnew – to bed, and spent the evening with those who had different degrees of understanding of 'Dad's serious night tomorrow.' Ironwood Jr. teleconferenced in. A family prayer, and a blessing upon all the children from their father, and they all, from the youngest to the eldest, went to bed calm and confident in the Lord, and knowing their father loved them.

That left Mrs. Agnes Hamilton, to hear what she had heard many times before.

"I have my insurance policies fully paid up, and I have faithfully kept up the additional savings account. I will be taking care of you, Aggie, no matter what happens. If you find a good Christian man who is willing to be a good stepfather to our children as well as a husband to you, just know I think that is the best thing you can do. You don't need my permission because death breaks all obligation you have to me, but just know: I don't take it as a betrayal.

"Junior is prepared now to take up the mantle of holding the business together with you; he and I discussed what will be necessary for the rest of the year. I also made up a list of orders and invoices so you won't have to think too much to keep things going.

"Just know this, Aggie: I love being here with you and the family, but I'm going to love being in the presence of the Lord even more. If tomorrow I go home there, grieve my not coming home here, but then move on. Get on with your life, and enjoy it as much as you can. Don't hold a torch for me.

"Lastly, my love, the choice is yours ... this night, what do you wish to remember me by?"

Mrs. Hamilton began to weep.

"My mind says that I'd love to sit around with you and listen to some nice music and drink lemonade and go down memory lane, because the last thing I would need as a widow is to be a widow with a new pregnancy. But if you are no more of this earth after Friday, and there is just one more chance of your legacy being in the earth through me ..."

"I've left enough insurance so that you and the rest can manage that 12th child, Agnes ... and if I make it, I'll be back early Saturday to raise him or her!"

"I just love you so much!" Mrs. Hamilton said. "Don't you know that's why you have 11 children? I've always had to let you go ... but I've been glad to make sure that you stay, too!"

"Oh, so that's what's going on! It's not because I'm irresistibly handsome?"

"That certainly doesn't hurt, but that isn't the reason! If you worked some regular job I would have been happy for us to tie some things and snip some others after Addison, but the chance to be constantly reminded of you in the faces and ways of our many children has sometimes been my only earthly comfort. I have missed you and will miss you so much!"

"You know, for a Yankee girl, you're very Southern traditionalist in your views about your man."

"Which is why you picked me!"

"Indeed," he said, taking her into his arms. "That's not the only reason, and I certainly would have considered stopping before 11 if I didn't feel the Lord could make it work for us, but I remember what you told me before my first deployment: 'Please don't leave me with just a memory.' Not that many women really want children nowadays, and to be frank, not that many men want that much responsibility, but all I know is responsibility, and so … ."

"And so we have had a wonderful, crazy life, founding our Hamiltown and taking it on the road," said Mrs. Hamilton. "I wouldn't trade for anything."

Captain Hamilton pulled his wife close, and kissed away her tears.

"I wouldn't trade either, and I don't intend to trade on Friday. But, just in case, let me leave you with a memory and more. Do you know what I really wanted to do on our wedding night, but I was afraid I would scare you?"

"What?"

Captain Hamilton picked his wife up and gently carried her to their room, closed the door, and then ripped his wife's gown and underclothes from top to bottom, clean off.

"There. That's better."

"Yep, that would have terrified me then," she said, "but I still would have liked it!"

"Well, now you have the memory, and you're about to get the rest!"

Lieutenant O'Reilly went to bed early, exhausted by all the work and all the interactions. He was too young to have rituals anticipating death, but he had sense enough to know he had a better chance of staying alive if he were well-rested.

Captain Lee went home and went through his rituals: he laid out his will, which named his beloved cousin and best friend Captain Hamilton as his primary heir, and laid out letters to his remaining immediate family and the family Lee, which was an entirely different prospect. He then laid out a special letter to the Morton family, of no account to Virginia but of great and dear account to him. He also laid out his requests for his funeral, including having his cousin Robert Wright Lee IV officiate, and Mrs. Hamilton to sing. He also left the next three months' rent for his landlord, so that his family would not have to hurry in cleaning out his apartment.

Lastly, Captain Lee took off the thin gold chain that he had worn around his neck for 27 years, a chain that held the amber ring he had given his wife, Vanessa Morton Lee. She had died with their son in childbirth when she, and then-Cadet Lee, were only 18 years old. He never wore that ring when he knew the next day's work might cause him to shed blood. She had not lived to know that part of his life save on the one occasion he had needed to defend her, and he had never regretted that.

When he went to bed, Captain Lee smiled. This had been the fifth time in two years that he had laid out things for his survivors, but the first time he had not picked up his revolver, loaded it, put it to his head, and then stood wrestling with the Spirit of God about pulling that trigger until the Spirit won the contest. This time, there was no need to wrestle.

"I am getting better," he said. "Lord, I thank You for sparing me in every way that You have done so, and being my Light in the midst of the darkness that has settled on me so often in these 27 long and terrible years. You are my Strength in my great weakness, my Song when all I want to do is weep – my Savior, in this life and the next, the One Who

163

gives me peace, and rest."

He felt it coming just a second before it happened; deep, restful sleep overtook him.

Chapter 11: The Gilligan House Stand

Friday morning, 4:45am: Captain Hamilton eased out of bed, very careful to leave his wife dreaming in the sweet afterglow of the love they had made the night before. That had always been his way. He left a letter for her, and also instructions for Addison, his oldest son at home, in case of his severe injury or death (although he knew that Adella, Agnes, and Iris would have to actually hold things down with their mother until Ironwood Jr. arrived), and then did an abbreviated version of both his isometrics and his shower before departing to his office.

Upon arriving and putting the coffee on, Captain Hamilton went out to get both the *Tinyville Times* and the *Lofton County Free Voice,* both of which were already out. They only agreed on one piece of news, and it was the critical piece: on this day, all police departments beside Tinyville, which had already complied with the Freedom of Information Act request, were going to comply, and the *Lofton County Free Voice* was going to do a public examination of the data at the Gilligan House.

6:30am: Lieutenant O'Reilly arrived at work with a grim face.

"We're really going to have to do this thing today," he said. "We almost need security at the Gilligan House now, some people are so angry about this."

"The fun won't start until the folks from the *Free Voice* arrive," Captain Hamilton said, "but if I were a betting man, I'd bet you even money that all of the fuming and fussing will be called off by then. Lofton County is big, but there aren't that many people in it, and if we're right about what we expect to come tonight, enough word will get out to calm the likes of Mary Leigh and her ilk down."

"Because someone else is going to take care of the problem," Lieutenant O'Reilly said.

"Exactly. Watch for it – we're going over there at about the time Mr. Varick should be finished with his rounds. Watch the body language of the others who will be looking on. Watch the way it will get eerily quiet toward sunset, as people clear out all around. Many will know, but nobody will witness."

"Which is why we are here," Lieutenant O'Reilly said. "Somebody has to witness, and stand against this evil."

"Exactly. That is the whole point of this day. Meanwhile, business as usual; we'll alternate checking on things at the Gilligan House every couple of hours."

Several miles away, another police officer in his office was tearing all the copies he had pulled down of the *Lofton County Free Voice* to shreds.

"Kindling!" he shouted to no one in particular. "Kindling!"

12:00 noon: Captain Hamilton got a phone call from Captain Lee.

"Are we on schedule?"

"Affirmative. Mr. Varick called me before he went down to Littleburg, and he ought to be looping back up to Big Loft in another hour and then through to Miniopolis and back here, to get to the Gilligan House at 3."

3:05pm: Mr. Varick returned to Tinyville, the little U-Haul he had rented full of files. He had checked them all before leaving the offices from which he had gotten them. He had stayed right in the police department offices where he had gotten the files while he checked, and had felt the hatred everywhere but in Big Loft, where Captain Lee was coolly professional, as always, and his subordinates dared not show any impatience.

Not everyone had such control of their subordinates, such as

Captain Bragg in Littleburg. One of his lieutenants had made the comment, "Oh, it's all there, Varick – for all the good it's going to do you."

Neither Captain Bragg nor Mr. Varick had visibly reacted, both of them knowing the import of the comment. It was now time for things done, not said.

A dozen willing hands were waiting at the Gilligan House for Mr. Varick and the files, including those of Mrs. James Varick IV, who greeted her husband with a hug and a kiss before taking up the clipboard and checking off the files before they were put back in the cases and the cases passed to another volunteer.

"Get on out of here, Ella," Mr. Varick said when they had finished. "It's going to be too hot even for your fine self around here in a little while."

"You better get home, Jim," she said. "I'm too beautiful to be anybody else's wife but yours."

"You most certainly are, Ella," he said, "and we don't intend to let that happen."

"The girls and I have not ceased to pray, and we'll keep praying."

"You had better be praying in Roanoke by 7 or so."

"I'll text you when we get there, Jim."

"Is Mrs. Harrison still being obstinate?"

"Marva is being marvelous, Harry, talking about she has an extra shotgun and knows how to use it. I've convinced her that the rest of us may need her on rearguard, so, she's heading up to Roanoke with us."

"You are as smart as you are beautiful, Ella. I'll see you on Sunday, Lord willing, and if not, see you after while."

He put his hands through his wife's salt-and-pepper twists, and kissed her bronze forehead before indulging in a long, sweet kiss of her full lips. Then she left, and he watched her strong, ample figure walking away with an appreciative shake of the head.

"I'm surely ready to meet You anytime You wish, Lord," he said, "but if You would leave me here to keep enjoying her a little while longer, I'd be happy too."

Then, he snapped himself out of it.

"Well, if You're leaving me here, it's to get the work You've given me to do, done," he said, and then drove the U-Haul back to the rental spot, picked up his car, and came back to the Gilligan House to start working with those files, along with 15 volunteers. Mr. Stepforth and Mr. Harrison arrived at about that time as well.

As darkness approached, Mr. Varick went upstairs to turn the lights and accessories on, then went back downstairs to finish the work of the day.

6:05pm: Captain Lee arrived from Big Loft in his pickup truck, and joined the caravan of the trucks of Captain Hamilton and Lieutenant O'Reilly. All-terrain vehicles were just a must, given the kind of work the night might bring.

6:30pm: A prayer and strategy meeting began at Roadside Southern Baptist Church – not the regular one, although some of its regular attendees were there. Men came from all over the county to attend. Wives came, and children. The mood was cheerful, if not exactly festive. A meal was served on the yard – a potluck. Good-looking fellowship, resembling a church meeting. It was not that, in the true Biblical sense of the church.

When the wives and children kissed their husbands and fathers goodbye, the men went on up into the choir room and changed – but not into choir robes, which at Roadside were brick red trimmed with cream. Their robes were white, as were their hoods. Here and there a sign of a hasty stitch, but, after all, they would only need these robes once before returning to their regular careers. Off they piled into their trucks and jeeps and cars, to get into position and wait.

10:00pm: As good as midnight in Tinyville. Stores and restaurants had been closed for an hour, and workers either at home or nearly there. The streets were empty, as were the side roads leading to those neighborhoods in which Tinyville began to blend with the countryside. The Gilligan House was in of those neighborhoods, very near where Tinyville officially ended. Lofton County proper officially began at the wood line, about two football fields' length from the back of the house.

Half of the white-robed men in the trucks began to get moving at 10:15; the other half stayed put, their guns trained on the back door and whoever might try to escape that way. It would be a veritable turkey shoot, from that perspective. The rest fanned out, cutting the phone line and covering the nearest cell phone tower.

Upstairs, the lights in the Gilligan House showed figures still moving back and forth, still working until the circuit breakers were shorted out, and thus plunged the house into complete darkness, a darkness then broken by the attackers lighting up their firebombs. One good firebomb to light up the front entrance, making that way impassible.

A brick and a firebomb, a brick and a firebomb, a brick and a firebomb through every window that could be reached – and if the throws through the upstairs windows fell short, they fell short in a way that set the exterior on fire too. All this was accompanied by a bloodcurdling cacophony of hoots and hollers and yells probably not attempted in Virginia since Nathan Bedford Forrest had ordered the KKK disbanded in the 1870s.

All this noise just to choke on it, with the fire at last growing bright enough to illuminate two silhouettes standing just by the front entrance – the long, tall, loose-limbed Captain Hamilton, his semi-automatic rifle trained on the leader of the white-robed mob, with Lieutenant O'Reilly right with him, covering his commander with his semi-automatic rifle.

"And that will about be all, gentlemen," Captain Hamilton shouted over the noise of the growing fire. "Give up now, and we've just got you for arson and attempted murder. Put those rifles down, back up, slowly, and get down on the ground, all the way down, hands splayed out."

Half of the men were so deflated they began to comply until the leader said, "Wait a minute – there are 87 of us and *two* of them."

172

"There are two of us that you can see, Captain Braxton Beauregard Bragg," Captain Hamilton said. "28 percent of the men of the town also wish you had the sense to just stand down."

There came such a sound of safeties coming off rifles from all around that half of Captain Bragg's mob put their rifles down and ran backward from them before getting down on their faces, their hands and arms splayed out like they were going to make snow angels.

"It's over, Captain Bragg. We already know about all the thefts you and others covered up by blaming Black folks. We already know about the kickbacks funneled down from Virginia's private prisons through the county prosecutor's office to the police departments that went along – every one of them in Lofton County. By 4:00am, it will be public news. But you and those with you don't have to be dead in that news. Stand down, gentlemen, and live."

"There's just two of them, no matter what it sounds like!" Captain Bragg shrieked. "Surely three of you have enough manhood to avenge yourself on him, after he took your livelihood from you!"

"Oh, those three worked with me long enough to know me," Captain Hamilton said. "They're already down – ain't that right, Lieutenants?"

"Yes, sir!" came three voices from the darkness.

Captain Hamilton wrapped his finger around the trigger of his gun.

"The stories, they say are written by the victors, Captain Bragg. You're not going to win this one. You are enjoying privileges you never gave any of the men you and your department railroaded, but even my patience is not limitless. I am going to say it for the third and last time: *Put down your weapons, back up, and get on the ground, while you still can do it willingly.*"

Another five men complied, leaving about 40 with Captain Bragg to make up their minds, but they too began to slowly comply, as Captain Bragg burst into a fit of swearing and weeping the likes of which had probably not been heard since April of 1865.

Yet Captain Bragg did not have the sense of his great-great-grandfather, to know when a thing irrevocably over was indeed over.

"I can't do it – I can't go down like this!"

The men still standing with him likewise picked up their weapons, and likewise died, in an orderly way. Captain Hamilton shot Captain Bragg and the man next to him; Lieutenant O'Reilly got the man to the other side of Captain Bragg, and those on either side of those dead by the side of Captain Bragg died in a hail of bullets that would have just as easily cut down 800 or 900 men, given enough time for men to move into position with newly loaded weapons.

The defenders of the *Lofton County Free Voice* had applied Captain Lee's deadly geometry from the deep shadows on the left and right sides of the Gilligan House. That geometry created a kill zone that even those who tried to get up and run found themselves victims of. However, Captain Hamilton and Lieutenant O'Reilly were safe just beyond the crossing of the lines, and doubly safe because they had jumped down into the trench dug for them to get below return shots. Not that there were any. Captain Lee's geometry had been brilliantly executed, with no mistake, by Mr. Turner and those with him.

Captain Hamilton and Lieutenant O'Reilly climbed out of the trench when the shooting paused – "All clear!" the captain shouted – and swiftly ran to the men that had sense enough to stay down. The two Tinyville officers had brought plenty of extra handcuffs, and the Black men who had come to the defense of their friends and neighbors brought rope for good hogties when the handcuffs ran out.

Meanwhile, around back, the men waiting in their pickup trucks realized something had gone wrong when no one came running out of the back entrance of the Gilligan House for them to shoot. Then they heard all the shooting from the sides and in the front, and knew something had gone wrong. They might have gone to the defense of their fellows, or they might have run for it, but they were not able to do any of that because not a single truck, jeep, or car would start.

"What in the – ?"

Of course they got out, and so were snatched, one by one and two by two, knocked out, and hogtied. The last man, in a growing and paralyzing sense of terror, was actually relieved to see the face of Captain Lee attached to the arm that quite suddenly reached through the window of his truck, pulled the gun out, and then pulled him right out afterward, clear through the window.

"Thank God it is you, Captain Lee," he said. "At least I know you won't just shoot me down!"

"Don't tempt me, Lieutenant," said his commander as he flung his subordinate to the ground. "I've been thinking about it since yesterday, you and your white sheet purchases, and coming into my office just smiling away like you had won the lottery! Well, you just did – the lottery for fools, which comes with an all-expense paid, indeterminate stay in one of Virginia's finest prisons!"

46 dead in the front, 41 handcuffed or hogtied; 32 hogtied in the

back, all caught up on arson and attempted murder – there was no hope of getting off, because Mr. Varick and the rest put down their weapons and rope and started identifying and snapping photos of the living and the dead. Random comments of the survivors and those who had defended their colleagues were put together with the two captains and Lieutenant O'Reilly's on-the-spot accounting, which in turn was backed up by the record of Mr. Turner's recorder, face up in the middle of the field of battle, poking out from under a rock that everyone coming down the field in front of the house had walked around. The information obtained was divided up amongst the victors, and so Captain Hamilton and Lieutenant O'Reilly had their reports to go write.

Captain Lee's night was not finished.

"Oh, I'm just good and warmed up," he said to his cousin Captain Hamilton. "I would be honored by your company as soon as the *Lofton County Free Voice* is posted up."

"Just warmed up, Colonel?" Captain Hamilton said. "We're about to do some Unit 6 things, I reckon!"

"And I need my humane adjutant to keep me from doing things the old way," said the former commander of Unit 6. "You remember that terrible recording the *Free Voice* obtained showing who the accessories are to this crime?"

"I do. If I were Commissioner Thomas or either of his two deputies, I wouldn't even try to defend this one – I'd fly with the dawn's early light."

"Which is why we are going to break their wings, in the darkest hour before the dawn they will ever see."

Henry Fitzhugh Lee was meticulous, including when and how he got hold of a judge in the middle of the night. The Honorable Joseph Bane Lofton Sr. was a fellow insomnia sufferer to the captain. The two had met in an all-night diner and hit it off, discovering in each other a love for justice and a hatred of corruption that had made close friends of them, despite the 20-year gap in their age.

"You would call on the one night that I was almost asleep, Lee," the judge had growled at his friend at 11:00 on Friday, "but at least if you are that hound that hunts all night, at least you have a juicy piece of game to offer me. As soon as you get me the report from the *Free Voice* and bring it to me, I'll write your warrants."

The second edition of the *Free Voice* for the week came out at 4:00am, printed on both sides because of all the news. In it, Mr. Varick had printed his transcription of the conversation the commissioner and his deputies had, and included a link to it on Facebook, accompanied by a live link of the Gilligan House *still* burning at 4:00. The imagery was powerful, but it was the words linking the commissioner and his deputies to the tragedy at the Gilligan House that was enough to get Captain Lee his warrants – at 4:15, since Mr. Nathan Turner drove up and handed Captain Lee a copy for the judge, right in front of the judge's house.

"Lee, you get on my nerves," Judge Lofton said at 4:30, in his robe, at the door, "but probably not as much as you are about to get on some other people's nerves."

"Thank you, Your Honor," Captain Lee said, and bowed.

"Thank me by getting off my front step, and not calling me for more warrants until noon. Go bother Danson; he'll be at work in his home office by 9."

"Yes, Your Honor. Thank you."

***

When you are the commissioner of police, or either of his two favorite deputies, the last thing you expect to hear is "POLICE! Open up!" between 4:00-5:00 in the morning. The last thing you expect is for the guilt of years of corruption to suddenly evaporate your courage like water suddenly under a blowtorch's flame, and for yourself to be running out of your back door in your underwear, or starting up your car and driving through your garage door in a desperate attempt to escape.

But, perhaps least and most ridiculous of all would you expect your last sight to be looking over the barrel of the gun of the man you had just hired four months before to solve all your problems. This was the ridiculously unthinkable end of Orton Thomas, commissioner of police in Big Loft, as the news of what he had conspired was spreading like wildfire across the county and burning as fiercely as the still-burning Gilligan House.

Commissioner Thomas had considered himself master of every situation as it came to hand. He was quick enough to realize that something had gone wrong with Captain Bragg's plan, and that somebody had traced it back to him – Bragg, had he survived, had probably wagged his tongue too much. He was also quick enough to figure out that only one man in his department was new enough to dare carry out some overzealous judge's order before dawn. It had to be Captain Lee.

Yet although he knew Captain Lee's record, the commissioner found Captain Lee in person to be brilliant but sad, slow to pick up on the subtle insults and pushback he was getting in the department on his cold cases, and exceedingly deferential to authority. So far, Captain Lee had not linked one of his cold cases to the Freedom of Information Act request– or so the commissioner had deluded himself. That delusion had led to others, each more damaging until the final, deadly one.

So, already in uniform for the day, the commissioner scrambled to the inside of his kitchen door, to wait, and was surprised to see the longer, looser figure of an officer in heather gray – backup from county? – in the foyer. That one was quick; his ears caught the commissioner's movement to fire and ducked behind a column in time to miss the commissioner's shot. However, the commissioner's shot at Captain Hamilton was followed by the commissioner's sudden awareness that someone was behind him.

That infamously handsome face, in all its cold, marble perfection, the muscle-packed and yet graceful figure, perfectly composed and posed … as near to a vision of the most deadly American of the 19th century as any Virginian of the 21st century would ever see, in his admittedly gorgeous mid-40s prime. Yet, if Commissioner Thomas in his last moments imagined General Lee had returned to Virginia, he swiftly had to come to terms with the fact that Lee had returned in his only fitting form for a warlike occasion: the Angel of Death, able to dispatch you at point-blank range no matter how well you, a mere mortal, mastered all events in the moment … except locking your back door, and thus allowing the partner of the officer you are shooting at from the kitchen to run up right behind you …

As for the two deputy commissioners, they ended up in various states of injury, having made the mistake of putting Captains Hamilton and Lee through the annoyance of having to chase them.

The first one had made it through his yard, closed his chain-link fence behind him, and locked it while his pursuers were running around the house. He figured that they would be slowed down. He wasn't ready when they both grabbed on to the fence at the top, pulled themselves up, jumped over, caught up with him, grabbed both his arms, and turned him right around, his legs still going, and slammed him right into that chain link fence.

"Very poor hospitality of you to slam that fence on us," Captain Lee hissed.

"Beneath the standards of any Southern gentleman," Captain Hamilton added.

He was hog-tied and thrown into the back of the cab of Captain Hamilton's truck, then seat-belted in because –

"Safety first," Captain Hamilton said.

The second deputy surprised his pursuers just a little by coming out of his garage without lifting the door, but that just was his writing his own invitation to a tailgate party sponsored by Captain Hamilton and his truck. Captain Hamilton just kept up until they were beyond the city limits, occasionally tapping the second deputy's car gently just to let him know he could get him at any time, while Captain Lee shouted on the bullhorn, "Pull over! Pull over, Pulliam, before I have to let you get hurt!"

Deputy Commissioner Pulliam wasn't listening, and so, once clear of town, Captain Hamilton got next to him and ran him off the road at 80 miles an hour, right into a field full of hay bales.

"It's amazing how much hang time those little cars get," Captain Lee commented as Deputy Pulliam's car landed in a huge hay bale, upside down.

Deputy Commissioner Pulliam was in tears by the time he was pulled from his car, hog-tied, thrown in next to his colleague Deputy Commissioner Solton, and also buckled up because –.

"Safety first," Captain Hamilton said.

That was the end, as dawn rose on a truly new day in Lofton

County. The sunrise was so beautiful that Captain Hamilton parked the truck for a few minutes on the last turn before rolling into Tinyville.

"It's just too beautiful to miss," he said, and Captain Lee smiled faintly.

After all, Captain Hamilton was the humane one, so much so that he could not begrudge anyone the last sunrise they would see for a few decades. The evidence seized from Commissioner Thomas's home showed that he and his deputies had colluded with Captain Bragg in the attempted murder of Mr. Varick and all staffers of the *Lofton County Free Voice* with him, while at the same time also destroying all the information they had given out.

For the time being, the two deputy commissioners would join their co-conspirators in the Tinyville jail until county belatedly sent to take them all to the county jail. Lieutenant O'Reilly had done a workmanlike job in getting everybody booked that was there before the two captains returned, with the muscle of 50 Black men from the town keeping the lieutenant safe from those he was booking!

The fire department had belatedly arrived at the site of the Gilligan House, and the fire would soon be out, but the house itself was gone.

"It went down in the service of our people – it died as it had lived, and that fate was better than some others about whom we could say the same thing," said James Varick IV when he and Captain Hamilton next spoke.

"Indeed," said Captain Hamilton. "A tragic night's work, but good work nonetheless. No casualties on our side, I trust."

"Just some minor injuries," Mr. Varick said. "A ton of work still to do."

"Always," Captain Hamilton said. "We both have a busy day and busy week ahead. I'm sure you'll want an official interview with me, and I'm available Monday for that."

"That will be fine," Mr. Varick said. "Thank you, Captain Hamilton. Give my thanks to Captain Lee and Lieutenant O'Reilly. Good morning."

"Good morning, Mr. Varick."

Next call: home.

"Woody?"

"Good morning, Aggie."

Captain Hamilton held the phone away from his ear because of the 12 Hamiltons, screaming for joy on the other end. When they calmed down a little, Captain Hamilton spoke again.

"It's a mess out here – it will be in all the news soon. I've got at least

12 hours of work to deal with before I can come home, but I'll be home, Lord willing, this evening."

Mrs. Hamilton lowered her voice to a sultry whisper.

"You know I'm going to be waiting on you, Woody, aching for that good old made-it-home-love..."

The ache instantly tore through the phone down her husband's spine, and made his head spin, his heart pound, and his mouth water ...

"Aggie..."

"Yes, Woody?"

"I'll be home in nine hours."

When he got home, ten hours later, Captain Lee likewise went through his homecoming rituals: his will, letters, and rent money went back into the lockbox designated for that, his gun went back into the locked closet for all such things, and then he went to his knees in thanksgiving and praise to God for his life and those who had fought beside him being preserved, and that "You restrained my wrath, so that I have by personal act and by strategic direction shed blood only in defense of myself and others who were worthy of defense, so that even those who opposed us but not fatally may live on to receive Your grace and mercy, even as You have shed it upon me, Whom You found in sin, but chose to deliver. I pray that You will grant repentance and saving faith to all who are in need who have survived this terrible night, and day."

Upon rising from his knees, Captain Lee changed into his street clothes, took his uniform out to be cleaned for pickup Monday, came home, made a reminder note to himself to call Mama Morton, made another reminder note for what to do with his time should he be placed on administrative leave, took his regimen of medicine with his limeade, turned on his Mozart through Monk playlist, drew himself a deep, hot bath, took off everything but put the gold chain with the amber ring back on, settled into his bath, and went to dreamless, restful sleep.

Lieutenant O'Reilly went home to bed, his being the simplest before-and-after ritual of all.

Chapter 12: Captain Hamilton Explains It All

In terms of police affairs in Lofton County after the Gilligan House Burning, Tinyville was the calm in the midst of the storm after the county had relieved its tiny jail of the crush of participants in that burning. Because Captain Hamilton had endured the (relatively) little storm of firing the last of the old guard and also completely submitting to the Freedom of Information Act request, Tinyville's direct consequences ended except, of course, for the loss of the Gilligan House. But, as Mr. Varick had said, the building had completed its purpose, and that long point of contention in the town also was ended.

Lieutenant O'Reilly found it eerily quiet by Monday as the storm that was destroying departments all over the county passed over Tinyville. Captain Hamilton had given his official interview to all the news agencies in the county and the region that morning, and it was just as calm and even and over much sooner than the lieutenant expected. The *Lofton County Free Voice* of course already had its news, and was there as a formality; the rest appeared to be completely in awe of the captain.

"Idol making is unfortunately a major pastime in Virginia, no matter the disaster," Captain Hamilton said later on. "It is our favorite coping mechanism, and, unfortunately, it gets in the way of us learning and growing through our experiences."

"I never thought of it that way, but, I suppose you're right," Lieutenant O'Reilly said. "I want to grow, sir. It … it hurt me so much, what happened, and how we had to fight our own colleagues. I looked up to many of them, but they were just stuck, and … I don't want to be like that, when I reach your age."

"That's half the battle won already," Captain Hamilton said.

"Let me explain this case to you in this way, Lieutenant. When I was a child, Lieutenant Sidney was in this office, and he made captain when I was in my teens. He was always kind to me, as kind as Captain Lee was to little Byron Berrier. I never saw him be unkind to anyone, of any color. If personal behavior was the mark of a racist, he never would have qualified. If that was my understanding of the matter, no one ever would have convinced me he was a racist.

"But I know better, and you must know better, Lieutenant. Whenever you see systems of racism at work, forget every idea of personal hatred. Remember first that Europeans decided to exploit North America and every person that was here, and grab out of Africa every person that they needed to do that. Racism is the justification that came later, but the decision to profit at everyone else's expense was made first. Thus, racism at work on a systemic level is the justification for a profit motive, always.

"When you see racist systems at work, there is always profit for the racists behind it. Find and root out the source of that profit, and you will have removed the nucleus of much of the corruption and crime that everyone in a region is suffering from, because any man that has so calloused his heart against one set of human beings that he can reduce them to chattel will do it to every other set he can, although his methods may vary.

"So: it was to that end that you have seen me crunching the data this office amassed on itself that showed the extent of the racism this office had indulged. Frankly I was too overwhelmed at first to clearly see the larger profit. My feeling was complete heartbreak, for I had loved Captain Sidney with a orphaned boy's trusting love for a father figure, but I had to work past that and with all the lieutenants until I could decide to keep you and put the rest out.

"My first clear thought was of the criminals still at large while Captain Sidney and his old crew were abusing the Black population of this town. Yet I did have the sense that there was something larger at work, and the behavior of our colleagues and former colleagues at our dinner at the Midway Bar and Grill alerted me that indeed, something was truly amiss. Their personal disdain for Black people I knew about. Their terror – especially Captain Bragg's – I did not. Captain Bragg was terrified, so terrified that he forgot not to needle Captain Lee."

Captain Hamilton sighed.

"I said to you after dinner on Friday that Captain Lee usually isn't growly. That's because his bark has never compared with his bite. Captain Bragg had known that for 40 years, since the two captains met for the first time as toddlers at a county-wide Vacation Bible School. Little Bragg loved picking kids small for their age to bully. He picked the wrong one in tiny Lee; his one push earned him a full-body tackle and body slam, a further slamming of his head several times into the dirt, and the perfect imprint of some baby teeth right by his darling little jugular."

"Even a baby pit bull is still a pit bull," Lieutenant O'Reilly said, shaking his head.

"You would think young Bragg would have learned from that. He didn't. Fast forward ten years. We were all in high school in Big Loft. Of course that high school was integrated by 1990, and white flight had taken place except for those of us white folks too poor for private school. We were outnumbered. Boyhood Bragg formed a brutal little gang – the BBB, with 'too young for the KKK but we're on our way' as the slogan. You see where that ended up this weekend."

"Yes, sir," Lieutenant O'Reilly said, shaking his head.

"Enter Vanessa Morton, whose beauty was described by her greatest admirer as 'petite perfect, dark as a summer night, kissed with the dew of stars.' She was as smart as she was beautiful, was a junior at 15, and beating out juniors a year older than her on the honor roll and in AP classes. That was disturbing to a lot of people. The administration didn't want it. A lot of the other kids of all colors were jealous. That made Miss Vanessa vulnerable, and the BBB moved in, mercilessly teasing and sliding into sexual harassment as they saw the administration was not going to stop them.

"However, Miss Vanessa's greatest admirer wasn't having that. Our now teenage pit bull was madly – and I do say, madly – in love with her, although too shy to confess it in the ordinary way. So, he made his feelings known by a heroic act of sheer insanity: taking on the whole BBB. He warned them and got her attention on the same day, while they were hassling her.

"Boyhood Lee still wouldn't hit his growth spurt for another two years. It didn't matter. He shoved two of the BBB members aside like they were straw weight and got right up in boyhood Bragg's face. He got up on his tiptoes and told his old enemy: you mess with Miss Vanessa again, runt Lee's going to whip you a *second* time, with all your little small-brained friends. He said it loud enough for everybody in the hallway to hear it. That was such a blow to boyhood Bragg, and such a shock to his crew, that they just watched as our favorite teenage pit bull picked up Miss Vanessa's books and offered to walk her to her bus stop.

"Well, at that point, everybody wanted the details of how big Bragg had been whipped the first time by runt Lee, and there were plenty who remembered and wanted to tell it. Of course, revenge was planned – and since boyhood Lee terrified the BBB, Miss Vanessa was the chosen target. Yet you know this possibility did not escape the mind of our teenage pit bull, what with his grasp of detail!

"First Friday of the summer: Miss Vanessa was coming from work, crossing a parking lot, about to get to the street and on the bus to meet the young man she was madly in love with for a secret rendezvous at Fruitland Memorial Park. The BBB pounced, and the harassment turned violent: Boyhood Bragg ripped open Miss Vanessa's shirt while the rest laughed. They had no idea that Miss Vanessa's young man had sensed the need to come and meet her at work, and was running up on them at that very moment.

"All at once, five of the seven members of the BBB were knocked clean out by the sixth, who had been grabbed by the ankles and swung around so his head knocked into their heads. That just left poor boyhood Bragg, bereft of his crew, to get worked over again."

Lieutenant O'Reilly shook his head.

"Probably only survived because Miss Vanessa was there."

"Correct, Lieutenant. Our teenage pit bull was too much of a gentleman to get blood on the clothes he was going to comfort his beloved in. So, he took boyhood Bragg's head and hand and let boyhood Bragg's car do the work smashing boyhood Bragg's face and hand. He then took his knife and avenged Miss Vanessa's humiliation by cutting boyhood Bragg's pants and underwear off, and then slung him through his own windshield and left him, backside on display to the world, bleeding from his broken nose and cut face all through his car's upholstery.

"Word spread fast. The BBB had terrorized a lot of young people. 'Runt' Lee became a hero to all of them. That is why West Point came looking for him."

"You mean to say the United States has some kind of scouting report?" Lieutenant O'Reilly said.

"A general with a background in Special Forces was at the mall where this happened," Captain Hamilton said. "He was on his way across the lot to rescue Miss Vanessa himself, but instead ended up watching how 'the little natural' handled that seven-on-one situation. Lofton County only had one public high school then, and of course the story was all over the place by the start of the next summer. That was how the United States of America's armed forces discovered the rise of another Lee.

"Obviously, Captain Bragg had paid for all of this in his second round of public humiliation! Self-preservation says you don't needle someone who had done that to you twice in 40 years, unless you have lost all sense of perspective. Captain Bragg had done so, evidenced by the way he was spouting off at Captain Lee at our dinner even after Captain Lee let him know he wasn't having it."

"That man had lost his mind," Lieutenant O'Reilly said. "I haven't known Captain Lee 40 days, and I would never have needled him."

"It takes no more than 40 minutes for most people to figure out it is not a good idea to needle Captain Lee," Captain Hamilton said with a grim smile. "Catch him in a really bad mood, and it doesn't take even 40 seconds. But when people are terrified, they lose perspective. Captain Bragg had just about lost his mind from terror over this Freedom of Information Act request, and that told me more was going on than had yet met my eye.

"Captain Lee and I compared our research into the data covered by the Freedom of Information Act request on Saturday. He and I knew about the money that the county wants to get from a huge private-public development partnership, but Captain Bragg's behavior tipped me off that more money was going into more hands. I knew, before the firing of your fellow lieutenants, that there were two dozen theft cases they had handled that clearly had not been committed by the people accused and convicted. I also knew there was no tracing of the return of the evidence or stolen goods, some of which were very valuable.

"I asked Captain Lee to take a look at his data about thefts and grand thefts, and he got back to me with the data he sent me and I shared with you about those 25 houses, including that braggadocios blue-and-gold atrocity owned by one Braxton Beauregard Bragg, Mr. BBB himself. You may ask yourself how he got a bigger house than

Commissioner Thomas, and there are two reasons: the former commissioner plowed his profits into stock, and he had to spread the wealth a lot more in Big Loft.

"But remember, in these small towns, the captains are what I am: captain, chief, and commissioner. Tinyville had a captain and four lieutenants; all of them had houses they couldn't afford on their salary, but that was done pretty early in the ten years asked for here. Littleburg, Miniopolis, and Shortport all had captains and lieutenants getting big houses all through the decade, as did Big Loft and the county."

"There was also the connection to the opening of a new private prison in Roanoke County, 11 years ago. Lofton County was feeding it heavily until it approached capacity about two years ago. Meanwhile, the captains and lieutenants started getting even bigger houses, as did the county prosecutor."

"So, that's what it was all about," Lieutenant O'Reilly said. "Bigger houses. The American dream."

"Which at no time has been achieved quickly by some without the great expense of others," said Captain Hamilton gravely. "It is also sadly true that people, having gained what they had no business having, wrap their whole guilty conscience and whole improperly inflated ego around it, and will kill in every direction to keep it.

"Captain Bragg tipped his hand Saturday on what he had in mind –
he kept making jokes about heat and fire and the next story and burning
… we all grew up in Virginia. We all know what that means.

"Captain Bragg had already said how he wanted to smash Mr.
Varick and Mr. Turner on his way into this office, and then said he was
on the phone talking to someone else. Captain Lee noticed his Bluetooth
blinking … and Bluetooths only do that when they are out of range of the
phone.

"Sure enough: Captain Bragg's car, and his phone, were down the
street and around the corner. He just happened to have the Bluetooth in
his ear, and thought fast enough to say he was on the phone … but
Captain Lee remembered how Captain Bragg loved to bully, and knew
that wasn't a figurative conversation.

"Captain Lee knew Commissioner Thomas had no desire to have
the Freedom of Information Act released in an understandable manner,
but not until last Tuesday did he suspect that the man who had hired him
was working with Captain Bragg on the plan to burn out the *Free Voice*.
He got the evidence on Wednesday, and it was some kind of evidence.

"You know that Captain Bragg asked for the phone numbers of

Commissioner Thomas and Sheriff Nottingham on Friday. We did not expect that to go well. Apparently, Sheriff Nottingham was not receptive; we caught relatively few county men this last Friday. Yet we caught a ton from Big Loft! Now, you know why."

"I don't remember booking Commissioner Thomas," Lieutenant O'Reilly said.

"That's because you didn't," Captain Hamilton said. "He is with his partner, Captain Bragg."

Lieutenant O'Reilly jumped.

"Captain Lee got him!"

"Captain Lee got both of them, really," Captain Hamilton said. "Remember: I was once a major, and he was once a colonel. I was once 'Colonel Lee's more humane adjutant.' Our counter strategy at the Gilligan House was his, with one exception. He told me that Captain Bragg and about half the men with him were not going to back down, and that it would be best to just stop all of them in the midst of their crime. However, Tinyville is our jurisdiction, Lieutenant. I decided to give as many of those men as possible a chance at life, though in prison.

"Remember: we have innocent men that need exoneration, doing time for crimes they did not commit. The admissions of the authors of the Gilligan House Burning in hopes of getting reduced sentences will do much to strengthen the work the Innocence Project will be doing to get the innocent men released and exonerated.

"Yet, I knew that Captain Lee was right. Captain Bragg and about half of his men would not back down. They couldn't. In getting caught at the Gilligan House, they would lose everything – career, reputation, all their gains for which they had thrown away their honor. They had nothing else to lose, especially Captain Bragg, in route to his third public humiliation in 40 years. Their egos would not let them back down. So: if we confronted them at the Gilligan House, we would have to kill them, either before or after. But there is a difference between killing 46 and killing 87, and, Captain Lee did it the way I wanted it in the back of the house, saving all of those men.

"Commissioner Thomas did not have to die, but it was inevitable after he started shooting back at me. I would have gotten him because the movement of his kitchen door would have given me half a second's advantage before he could shoot at me again, but, he had also left his back door unlocked."

Lieutenant O'Reilly shook his head.

"Captain Lee got behind him, point-blank range, just that quick."

"Yes, young sir, that is precisely how it happened. By contrast, the commissioner's deputies were just laughable, so we didn't hurt them too bad. They will give up a lot of useful information that the *Free Voice* and the Innocence Project will be able to make good use of."

"How did Mr. Varick and the others from the *Free Voice* escape the burning?"

"Recall that the Gilligan House was a stop on the Underground Railroad. Extra rooms, a hidden passage underground into a little shack in the woods. It was cobwebby, but usable, so, Mr. Varick and company took the files out at once to safekeeping and to the people truly designated to work with them, and then stripped the house of all the historical objects that could be rescued. We put up a projector to show images of people moving around the upstairs, but the house had been empty several hours before we took our positions."

"Wow," Lieutenant O'Reilly said. "The authors of the Gilligan House Burning never had a chance."

"When members of the community and honest police officers find a way to work together, most criminals don't stand a chance," said the captain. "We cannot do anything about the history that makes it so hard to do that. But, we were granted that possibility last week, and then went and appropriated the possibility and made it come to reality. That is now new history for Tinyville, which I pray mightily that we can build on correctly to get to a future much different from this region's past. Pray and work; work and pray; that's all there is to it. Oh, and lunch. There's also lunch."

Lieutenant O'Reilly smiled.

"Is what I think it is in the refrigerator?"

"Yes, young sir, I went on and ordered from the Midway Bar and Grill last night for today – I trust you and I can have a good meal free of hidden terrors. Save room for the pound cake, too."

Epilogue 1: Interview with the Angel of Death

In the life of many persons and institutions, there comes a moment of contact with a person or persons that forces a rethink of life and a re-examination of even the most deeply held beliefs.

Such a moment was inevitable for the new acting commissioner of police after the Gilligan House Burning weekend. Nobody had gotten around to putting Virginia's very own Angel of Death on administrative leave, and the angel was coming back to work on Monday ...

In brief: the Gilligan House Burning had occurred because a *bunch* of rogue officers from Big Loft – including the commissioner and his two deputies – had conspired with a whole bunch of rogue officers across Lofton County to destroy the *Lofton County Free Voice* newspaper and all the information it had demanded and received on incidents and arrests involving Black citizens of Lofton County.

The captain of police in Tinyville, VA, where the Gilligan House was located, wasn't having it. Ironwood Hamilton had worked with the *Free Voice* and the 28 percent of Tinyville that had an interest in the *Free Voice* to figure out what was going on and to plan and successfully execute a counter-strike. The Gilligan House had been lost in the process, but so too had been 46 rogue officers, with 73 more captured and jailed.

That left Commissioner Thomas of Big Loft and Deputy Commissioners Solton and Pulliam, comfortably in their beds as the *Free Voice* put out a recording they had received showing how the commissioners had conspired with the captain of police in Littleburg to arrange the attack on the Gilligan House … comfortably asleep until the man they had agreed to hire as a new captain went and got warrants, snapped up the two deputies, and killed the commissioner while he was resisting arrest!

No one had seen that coming. The new captain was indeed a marble model gentleman of the old cut, quiet and unassuming, coolly calm and composed, and with a profound capacity for work. He was deferential to authority as befit his military training, respectful to his peers, and firm yet intensely supportive to his subordinates, although all of this showed more in his actions than his few words.

Only if you thoroughly knew the histories of the Revolutionary and Civil Wars and then looked carefully at the new captain's service record since his graduation from West Point might you realize that there might be much more to Colonel Henry Fitzhugh Lee, in his new career as police captain, than the marvelous marble mask that met the eye.

Acting Commissioner Pendleton's head spun as he considered the sequence of the week before the Gilligan House Burning. On Tuesday, Commissioner Thomas had invited Captain Lee out for a drink, and according to the commissioner it had gone very well, although the captain had only ordered a fancy limeade. On Wednesday, Thursday, and Friday, the two men had interacted professionally and courteously, many, many times around the Woodard case and the release of the Freedom of Information Act materials.

Not that everything had been sunshine and roses to that point. Despite his gentlemanly manners, Captain Lee had made plenty of enemies. He had closed a case left open for 24 years in his first full week on the job, and from then on averaged closing a case every 10 days. His closes were brilliant, and his expositions of how things actually fit together were flawless.

The problem was that Captain Lee thus showed up every officer who had worked those cases before him, and the department as a whole. His brilliance overcame the coldness of the cases, but the speed indicated that others could have closed those cases in a reasonable time with a little more attention to their work. This led to the question of what folks had been doing all that time, a question made exceedingly dangerous when the *Lofton County Free Voice* requested the information that contained the answers.

Then, Commissioner Thomas had handed that same Captain Lee access to that ten years of reports and associated data for the Freedom of Information Act request the *Free Voice* wanted on incidents and reports involving Black citizens. Wiser heads had advised the commissioner not to do that, but he ignored them, not wishing to believe (despite the abundant evidence Captain Lee had put up in his second army career in the Judge Advocate General wing) that an officer so good at small cold case puzzles would be equally good at solving the big puzzle of why Big Loft's police department was so inept in some areas and so *efficiently wrong* in others.

Terrified but also mastered people – for even with his mild-mannered ways, Captain Lee was still just as obviously the kind of man you didn't dare cross – have limited options. Obstruction, and gossip: those were the two biggest ones.

Still, Captain Lee walked above it all. He never complained about anyone, always found complimentary things to say about his fellow officers and their work, always gave scrupulous attention to orders from above and in passing those orders down, always passed credit around and took responsibility for what he could have done better. He remained the consummate professional officer of middle rank, always, and kept closing cases, week after week after week.

Thus, the commissioner had been mostly comfortable – mostly, because he relieved himself of his deeper fears by occasionally engaging in the silliness of gossip around Captain Lee as well. After that Thursday morning, the commissioner had convinced himself: all would be well. Even General R.E. Lee ultimately had been contained; his great-great-great nephew H.F. Lee would pose no exception. The department would get over the Freedom of Information Act bump, and back to business as usual soon enough.

The commissioner was wrong, of course. The Freedom of Information Act bump was not to be gotten over after the Gilligan House Burning, and, business, whatever the new norm was going to be for it, would go right on without Commissioner Thomas in the world to be part of it.

The man who had ushered his boss into eternity was in his office on Monday morning, probably juicing his lemons and limes, doubtless deep in his data-crunching … working because *nobody* had told him not to come to work. Dutiful man was H.F. Lee, dutiful, inscrutable, and, even as a glorified data manager in what should have been a quiet, bloodless job, still worthy of his nickname on both sides of the Army he had spent 23 years in: the Angel of Death.

"What am I going to do about it?" Acting Commissioner Pendleton said to the walls of his new office. "The last three bosses that crossed him are in jail or *dead!*"

The Fear of Lee, come home to roost in Virginia, was a real and terrible thing.

***

Between the constant pressure of the press and boxing up Commissioner Thomas's things and trying to comfort the utterly hysterical Mrs. Thomas and her 24 counterparts, Monday went right by Acting Commissioner Pendleton. When he came in the next day, he went and checked who had clocked in. Captain Lee had clocked in at his usual time: 7:45am, early enough to greet the night crew and janitors as they departed, to greet the day staff and get the freshest coffee, to leave nice notes for staffers who had been helpful to him the day before, and to get settled in before the the general rush of day shift arrival.

By the time the acting commissioner arrived, the captain had been entrenched for two hours already, the wake of his presence still visible in the happiness of the staffers whose smallest contributions had been recognized, and the preternatural calm of the small hallway leading to his small office, out of which issued the captain's choice of music, or, periodically, a junior officer, full of encouragement and confidence, going to carry out the captain's orders.

Acting Commissioner Pendleton thought about going down that hallway to Captain Lee's office and telling him to turn off his computer, put his badge and gun on the desk, turn in his door fob to security, and not to return unless and until sent for. Yet the acting commissioner's feet ran the exact opposite course from his head, and he found himself in his office not even knowing how he had gotten there.

Tuesday got away. So did Wednesday and Thursday. Acting Commissioner Pendleton was running around like a man trying to put out a fire with a toy pail of water – the department was short 42 men under the worst imaginable circumstances, and the press would not let up. The *Big Loft Bulletin* by itself would have been bad enough, but it and the local TV news stations were being led around by the *Lofton County Free Voice,* which had started kicking the Big Loft police department where it really hurt. The paper had the Freedom of Information Act data to show why the department's top men had gotten involved a criminal conspiracy to destroy the paper, and the paper started putting it out, every day of the week, along with its other related stories.

All the while, Henry Fitzhugh Lee came to work at 7:45am, left at 5pm, and then filed a report on Thursday showing that he estimated closing the Godfrey case by Friday – eight days after closing the Woodard case, without even a procedural hiccup caused by the Gilligan House Burning and all that went with that. Captain Lee was on schedule, while everything was collapsing around him and he was part of the reason for the collapse.

At last, this was too much for the acting commissioner. On Thursday at 6pm, when he returned after a grueling day to the office and found a copy of Captain Lee's newest report, he said to the report everything he wanted to say to the person who had written it, in a tirade of cursing and swearing not heard in the office since segregation had ended in Virginia. After that, the acting commissioner began to make phone calls – something was going to have to be done.

***

Acting Commissioner Pendleton got up early on Friday just to observe

... the Angel of Death walked to work most days, and sure enough, around the corner he came at 7:35am, his long stride efficient but unhurried. He had ten minutes to work with at that point, and took two minutes of that time to carefully remove a copy of the *Lofton County Free Voice* from the community poster board across the street, fold it twice, put it in in his inside pocket, and then cross back to the side the station was on. He then waited, and then smiled, broadly, as a little old woman, well-dressed and looking purposeful though slow-moving, came to the corner.

"This is the part of my day that encourages me the most!" she said. "Thank you for always being here, Captain Lee!"

"My pleasure and honor, Judge Brown," he said gently, and offered his arm to her to help her across the street and then up the steep stairs into the county courthouse.

Acting Commissioner Pendleton shook his head at that. No wonder Captain Lee could get warrants quickly – he was cultivating the right relationships in town! Judge Joseph Bane Lofton, and also Judge Lorelei Brown ... two of the most influential senior jurists in the county and the state. Who else had Captain Lee cultivated? It was a terrifying thought.

Four minutes left: Captain Lee came lightly down the courthouse stairs and again crossed the street, and then walked into police headquarters, tagging his fob to the proper place – clocked in, 7:45am. After that and only after that – 8:00am – did the men from Internal Affairs arrive to start looking over the situation. The acting commissioner wanted everything arranged before bringing Captain Lee to face them.

8:45am – new problem. The *Free Voice* that day had released names of Big Loft officers involved in some of the worst of the harassment and false arrests of Black citizens in the city. None of them were on administrative leave. The protesters and reporters from all available news agencies were in front of headquarters by 8:45. The protesters began reading the passages from the *Free Voice* aloud for the rest of the press. Everybody coming to work at the regular time had to wade through that to start their day – including some of the men whose firing the protesters were clamoring for.

Inside, the acting commissioner spent half of his day getting that whole situation under control, including interviewing the officers named and putting *them* on administrative leave.

Finally Captain Lee was summoned; the acting commissioner could hardly believe his own ears as he said into the phone, "Captain Lee, could you just please step over to my office when you have a convenient moment?"

The men from IA stared in surprise, but, they didn't understand – yet.

If Captain Lee had not had a convenient moment until the world ended, the acting commissioner had just given him an out. However, his response was typical: "I am even now on my way, Commissioner."

It took all of five minutes – the door of the office was open – before Captain Lee's measured step was heard on approach, and he was glimpsed through the door, in the secretary's office outside. Just at that time, there was a woman's cry, and the sound of many things beginning to fall. Captain Lee's figure darted to his right, and the falling noises stopped.

"Oh, Captain, thank you!" cried Ms. Thornton, the commissioner's surviving secretary. "I've been telling people that this serving table for coffee and refreshments has been literally on its last legs for weeks, but nobody in grounds and facilities has been paying attention! That would have been such a mess, and I just can't take any more messes right now!"

She almost started crying ... this third secretary of the late Commissioner Thomas had been too honest to be in with the in crowd that had gotten to go to casual lunches … but her honesty had saved her from being snatched up in his fall. Captain Lee had concluded she had not partaken in the many, many schemes coming out of the commissioner's office in the two years she had worked for him, and so she was not in jail and was still at work.

Captain Lee was deeply impressed by the character of the one honest person in the heart of the corruption he had destroyed, and knew that she had suffered much – too much to deal with a collapsing table.

"My pleasure and honor, ma'am," he said gently. "While I am holding this end of the table, move the heavier items off, and it will balance itself. Then, put those items back here, and here. The table will hold up a little while longer, and I will call down to grounds and facilities on your behalf."

"OK … oh, my, that worked well!"

"Do you have copies of what you sent to facilities and grounds, and how long ago you began sending?"

"Yes, sir, right here. I'll just dial the number when you are ready."

"I am ready now, thank you … good afternoon. This is indeed Ms. Thornton's desk but this is Captain Henry Fitzhugh Lee speaking. With whom do I have the honor to speak? Mr. Tobias Marsh? Good afternoon, Mr. Marsh. I am on my way to the commissioner's office, but had to turn aside to spare Ms. Thornton serious injury and the outer office serious need for cleaning because this table she has been asking to have replaced for several weeks is not replaced … No, Mr. Marsh, I am not going to do another requisition in writing because you have nine requisitions in writing from Ms. Thornton, and you have kept her waiting, in clear and present danger to both her and the commissioner and his guests, for five weeks, two days, four hours, and fifty-five minutes. You have exactly five minutes to get that table here, Mr. Marsh, before I come down and find out why it is not here."

When you are accorded the status of the Angel of Death by folks doing wrong, those folks don't want a visit from you. Five minutes later, just as Captain Lee checked his watch, two men from grounds and facilities came in with Ms. Thornton's new serving table, and in ten minutes, she was all set up again and happy.

"Captain Lee, you are an angel!"

"Since the word for angel is really an old word for messenger-servant, I accept your sweet compliment in the spirit in which you intend it, ma'am."

"I'd kiss you, but we're on duty!"

Captain Lee checked his watch with a smile.

"Two hours, fifty-nine minutes to wait."

Ms. Thornton giggled and blushed.

"Oh, Captain Lee, you're so timely and sweet! Anyway, the acting commissioner is in, with some other folks."

"Thank you, Ms. Thornton."

Captain Lee then headed for the inner office, but stopped as he heard what everyone else heard – rapid footsteps coming toward the outer office, and a door flung open.

"Captain Lee! Captain Lee!"

The captain turned around in the doorway of the inner office.

"Yes, Lieutenant Longstreet?"

"You were right, sir – I followed up on that tip you gave me, and found old Mrs. Goddard in a tiny nursing home in Smallwood! She's willing to be interviewed from her hospice bed!"

"Go do the interview, Lieutenant."

"What? But I thought –?"

"Under normal circumstances I would do it, but there is a reason I have spent half the week preparing you to do it if the tip bore fruit. I may be placed on administrative leave, in which case Captain Hayes will have to take over the Florence case. But he cannot get to it until Monday.

"Mrs. Goddard is dying, Lieutenant – her condition and medications are constantly in flux and trending downward. There is no guarantee she will be in condition to think and speak clearly or even be alive by Monday. So, you go do it, Lieutenant, and report to me if I am still here or to Captain Hayes on Monday. I have every confidence in you: go do it."

"Yes, sir, Captain Lee!"

Lieutenant Longstreet went running, only to be recalled by his captain.

"Do you have your digital recorder, Longstreet?"

"I'll go to my desk and get it."

"Save time. Here's mine."

"Oh, wow – thank you, sir, yes, indeed, I'm going now!"

The footsteps retreated as swiftly as they had come, and at last, Captain Lee turned around and faced those who were about to decide his professional fate.

"My apologies, sirs. A break in the Florence case, at last."

Handshakes and introductions all around, while the acting

commissioner's discomfort grew and the IA men began to understand. It was like the day Captain Lee had come in for his interview; he was cordial and easy of manner, but you just knew he had sized everyone up before he sat down to talk, and knew he could take or leave them. At some point in that sizing up, he had decided he could take any one of those men to the grave if necessary. All the men presently in that office knew that, and it destroyed the power dynamic they should have enjoyed.

The acting commissioner and the IA men had their questions ready; they had made sheets up, sheets that they suddenly were too sheepish to show. Something about Captain Lee, and the easy way he drew out his pencil and notepad, unnerved them.

"Oh, you won't need those, Captain," the acting commissioner said. "I don't have any orders, exactly. We just want to ask a few questions about last Saturday."

"Yes, sir," Captain Lee said. "I stand ready to answer any questions you may have, Commissioner and gentlemen."

No statement could have been made more appropriately, in a more mild-mannered way. There was nothing in his body language that betrayed any sign that he was acting a role. Yet it was the exact same answer he had given during his interview – and four months later, he had destroyed three of the seven men who had heard him say it the first time.

It would be four, in the end, for Acting Commissioner Pendleton did what everybody knows you're not supposed to do with the Angel of Death. On the other hand, you can't interview someone without looking them in the face, and in the eyes.

The vision was among the most beautiful any Virginian could hope to see, of a handsome and idolized face come once again to life, in calm, peaceful repose, the marble slightly tinted with lively rose, the dark eyes bright, the firm mouth, square chin, and huge cranium as solid as one might have imagined them being, the hair still mostly dark because of youth, for this Lee was in still in his middle forties.

Yet since one had to accept that this Lee, meek and mild on a Friday afternoon, had swept away three of his superiors and a goodly portion of his department six days and 12 hours before, and *still* could present this meek and mild, then one had to accept other realities ... how Washington, and Jefferson, Madison, and two Lees could have been mild-mannered gentlemen, loving to their friends and loved ones, generally personable to everyone they met, and *still* brutalizers of their slaves – torturers, rapists, pedophiles, *murderers,* and, at the last, *traitors* to their own nation in a futile attempt to maintain the right to *continue*

219

brutalizing Africans in America.

To Acting Commissioner Pendleton, the world as he understood it – including his own proudly held view of Confederate General Pendleton, his great-great-grandfather – depended on things being just one way. His foreparents had to be heroes, gentlemen, patriots, loving fathers and husbands – all that was good. Admit for one moment that Black people were right, and that accurate historians in the North and West were right – accept any evidence that such men could be *all* of what they were described as being, and the whole thing went up like a puff of smoke.

Captain Lee was looking back across Commissioner Pendleton's desk. The colonel-turned-captain – this exceedingly mild-mannered modern officer and gentleman who in a night turned on and swept away the most powerful men in his own department when they crossed the line – was *real*. This was the true cause of the personal terror the acting commissioner felt about Captain Lee. Accept the modern Lee for *all of it,* and one also had to accept his ancestors and Virginia and America for *all of it.* He was living, breathing, irrefutable evidence of how that all could be – and was – true.

One hour later, Lieutenant Longstreet returned to find Captain Lee at his desk, writing his report on the close of the Godfrey case.

"What happened, sir?"

"You tell me – what did Mrs. Goddard have to say?"

"She said everything you said she was going to say! She killed Mr. Florence and had that trailer park built over and around him after filling his shallow grave with formaldehyde from Mr. Goddard's job, and she said she killed him because he was molesting her great-niece and nobody in the family was willing to turn him in!"

"That was what the evidence suggested," Captain Lee said, "and is the only explanation that fits the facts. How long does she have?"

"The doctor says she has until Wednesday."

"Transcribe the interview now and write your report Monday, and when she dies, we will officially close the Florence case."

"Yes, sir."

"Well done, Lieutenant Longstreet."

"Thank you, sir – but what happened? You're still here. What happened with Commissioner Pendleton and Internal Affairs?"

"Just as we were about to begin, the acting commissioner pitched forward over his desk, unconscious."

"Did he make it?"

"Sadly, Lieutenant, he did not. He died right in front of us, of a massive heart attack."

Captain Lee sighed heavily, and his marble composure dissolved into a look of sorrow.

"It has been a terrible week," he said, "and my decisions are a large part of how terrible."

Lieutenant Longstreet looked both ways and behind him, and Captain Lee reached over and turned up the volume on the Piedmont Blues.

"That's why you keep all that on?" the lieutenant said, with a slight smile.

"Partially," the captain said. "It serves many purposes."

The lieutenant sat down at the other side of his captain's desk, and spoke in a low voice.

"Somebody had to do it, Captain Lee. Somebody had to. When I came here a year ago, I thought police work was about community and justice and doing the right thing. Then I came here, and the corruption and weakness were suffocating. The turnover in this department is huge because of it.

"I was going to leave, but then, you came, Captain Lee, and you weren't about feathering your own nest, but about getting things done right. Many hate you here, because of that, but I and a bunch of others feel differently, and our feelings didn't change last weekend. Somebody had to do it, Captain Lee. Too many people have been getting away with too much for too long. Somebody had to do it, and I thank God that it was you."

Captain Lee's face suddenly colored up in a flush of strong emotion. He did not say anything for a few minutes, but the lieutenant could tell he had touched something deep inside his senior officer's soul.

"Lieutenant," he said at last, "what you have said makes the consequences no easier, but that they are easier than what came before, for you and your oncoming cohort of young officers, does provide me some much-needed perspective."

The bud of a smile touched his lips.

"Well, since we will both be here at least through Monday, I had better finish my report and you had better transcribe Mrs. Goddard's confession with your notes. When that is done, we can get out of here and rest this weekend before tackling Donato and Keys."

"Actually rest this weekend – sounds good to me, Captain."

"And to me also, Lieutenant, believe me!"

Epilogue 2: The Fall of Roadside Baptist Church

For any pastor, a last sermon is always a difficult task, but if you and the congregation in that situation are *both* being put out, that is a real challenge.

This was the challenge in the wake of the Gilligan House Burning that Rev. Theodore Willborough had to face at Roadside Baptist Church.

Roadside had certainly been through its struggles already. It was the product of the collapsed Baptist churches of both Tinyville and Littleburg in Lofton County, VA, merging together with difficulty after the leaders of both churches found themselves bidding on a big plantation house that was halfway along the country road between the two towns.

Neither church had money enough to make the purchase, but they had been hyping the purchase to their members and encouraging them to give while the Lord made a way, and each church saw the other as the Lord making that way.

Never mind that each church had collapsed before that because they had refused the leading of the Lord to reach out to the community as it existed – 39 percent Black – and as it was changing. A growing number of Latino fieldworkers had been settling in since the 1980s, and the county was becoming younger in all racial groups.

Never mind that each church had fiercely clung to its own traditions and resisted all change both within its doors as it did in its towns, meaning that once a merger took place and the two churches had to change to accommodate each other, that, too, would be resisted or the new church would be abandoned by many members. Its ability to exist would be tenuous at worst and eventually compromised by attrition unless the Spirit of God took control – but He, too, was still being resisted.

Thus, the perfect storm had hit Roadside Baptist Church on the day of the Gilligan House Burning. The change to be resisted was the coming of the *Lofton County Free Voice,* a new and confrontational Black newspaper that had called out the entire county and all its police departments in its first issue.

The *Free Voice* also had its plans to fill future issues: its Freedom of Information Act demand for records about how the police departments had been treating Black citizens in the towns, big city, and county over ten years.

The *Free Voice* would have messed up the lifestyle of a lot of the members of Roadside Baptist Church. Somehow, in the same decade which the Freedom of Information Act covered, a whole bunch of police officers had been improving their standard of living for themselves and their families – and improving their offerings – in a manner beyond their salaries. It was just called the favor of God. Yet the favor of God would not at all have been endangered by the *Free Voice.*

Roadside's legacy was the combination of two churches that had been a haven for those who resisted change – in the context of Tinyville and Littleburg's churches, there had been many occasions in which old terrorists like the KKK had met and found comfort and shelter in the trappings of church.

Thus, it was new and not new to Roadside when the 119 men who would participate in the Gilligan House Burning met there the very day for fellowship and a potluck. It was new and not new to Roadside that the men at last, when the sun was down, went up into the choir room to change into the white pillowcases and sheets their mothers, wives, daughters, or girlfriends had lovingly tailored for their weekend moonlighting as domestic terrorists. Everyone expected these men to remove their sheets, rest on Saturday, put their church clothes on Sunday, and return, as if nothing had happened.

What was new to Roadside was its new young pastor, Rev. Theodore Willborough, who did his best to preach the whole counsel of God including what the Scripture speaks of in the Epistles concerning Christian conduct, Scripture that denies the Christian any liberty to righteously participate in any kind of racist behavior.

Rev. Willborough spoke against pride of face and pride of race, and of malice of all kinds being of the flesh and not of the Spirit. He spoke of the oneness all Christians enjoyed in Christ without regard to race or background, and of the affront to Christ it was to mistreat one's Christian family and the neighbors to the Christian family outside the church.

Rev. Willborough was tuned out because of his youth. Roadside would have replaced him if it could have afforded to do so, but it couldn't. He was the only pastor who would or could serve at that rate. So, the membership enjoyed when he preached on subjects that it liked, and tuned him out when he didn't, feeling that sooner or later he would mature into understanding that some things were just the way they were, and if the Lord had wanted them stopped, He would have stopped them.

Thus, Roadside was sent a man new to it and not new to it. Major Ironwood Hamilton, U.S. Army Reserve, whose family had attended

Tinyville Baptist Church when he was a child, returned to Tinyville at the invitation of the town to become its new police captain. Captain Hamilton had immediately begun attending the successor to his old church, and when he had been able to move his family down to Tinyville, he had brought them there.

However, Captain Hamilton and others were discontent, resonating greatly with the less popular sermons of Rev. Willborough and grieving that the old problems that had destroyed the old churches were still alive and well in the new church.

Captain Hamilton had begun to talk with some of those who were unhappy, and by the Sunday before the Gilligan House Burning, they had begun to consider founding a new church in Tinyville. The decision was made that they would seek God in prayer, and count on God to show them what they were to do, and when.

Then had come the fateful Friday, on which night Captain Hamilton made his stand before the Gilligan House, and with those with him killed 46 and captured 73, accounting for all 119 men who had gathered at Roadside just four hours before.

It did not take long for Captain Hamilton to find out that there were 35 men from Littleburg and 10 from Tinyville among the dead and wounded, and that of those 45 men, 25 were regular attendees of Roadside Baptist Church, including the head deacon who had given permission for the 119 to use the church for a rally before coming out to burn the Gilligan House.

Those 25 men represented one-tenth of Roadside Baptist Church, one-fourth of its men, and *65 percent* of its "anchor contributors."

Those 25 men represented 25 families who were now bereft of their breadwinners by one means or another, in the worst way – overextended because of the bloat of the proceeds of police corruption and with absolutely no way to maintain the income necessary to maintain their lifestyle. Housing, medical care, childcare, education – *all of it* – became impossible in a single night for 25 families in Roadside. Funeral costs were equally out of reach for 12 of them.

Those 25 families represented the margin of Roadside playing *its* bills, month to month. With their support gone, Roadside was instantly insolvent, scarcely able to pay its bills through the end of the week, not able to make it through the month, to say nothing of being able to make the mortgage payment on the building.

No survivor in the church leadership even bothered to call Rev. Willborough, who was in Richmond with his family after the funeral of a great-aunt. Captain Hamilton had called.

"Pastor, I know you are with your family," he said, "and you know you have my condolences and sympathy. I wouldn't call unless it was an emergency."

An hour later, Rev. Willborough was tearing down the highway toward Tinyville, having caught up on the afternoon news after hearing what the captain had to say.

On that terrible Sunday, Rev. Willborough knew that a lot of members would be missing – Captain Hamilton himself was dangerously exhausted, for example, and more than 25 families would be in shock and grief. So, he decided to turn the entire day over to prayer, and prayed with hundreds of people from Tinyville and Littleburg who came to the church for comfort. Afterward, he visited every absent family he knew of, ending with the Hamilton family that evening.

The Hamiltons, one and all, made their pastor very much at home, which made the unavoidable conversation between the pastor and the captain easier after Mrs. Hamilton had directed the rest of the family to other pursuits.

"I need to know what happened, Captain Hamilton," he said. "Give it to me straight. I have to take it, so the Lord will enable me do so."

Captain Hamilton had spared no detail, to Rev. Willborough's horror. He had finished with some chilling warnings.

"Legally, you are the CEO of Roadside Baptist Church, Pastor, which is a 501c3. Several members of your board of trustees and deacon board were involved in the rally before the burning, so many that it could be construed that the church, in contravention to its tax-exempt regulation, is a co-conspirator in a criminal act that resulted in the death of 46 men.

"I am not going to pursue that angle on the criminal side, but you need to prepare for the possibility for challenges to the church's status, and also civil lawsuits as the 25 families in the church who are now without their primary breadwinners look desperately for resources. People who would encourage the destruction of one house for something of little direct effect upon them might certainly destroy their own church house when their survival is at stake."

"Well, there's not much to destroy," the pastor said wearily. "We are two years into a 30-year mortgage, and, although I will not know until tomorrow, we are probably insolvent as of the end of the month. Those that would profit from it would have to move very fast for very little."

"The people who did the Gilligan House Burning decided on their course of action and coordinated how they would carry it out in *18 hours*," Captain Hamilton said. "Those who they have led and molded intimately, and who encouraged them in their murderous ways, are still part of Roadside. You had better have a plan to deal with that reality as quickly as the Lord will illuminate your mind with that plan."

***

Rev. Willborough could not sleep that night, so he got into his car and drove up to Big Loft to the Wide Eyes Diner, famous for its 24-hour service and their midnight pancake specials. It also had great coffee, which was not really a good thing if you couldn't sleep, but if you had decided to utilize the time and go to sleep later in the morning, the coffee was just right.

Rev. Willborough was doing something he had liked to think real ministry would never involve: crunching numbers. He knew the numbers for the church: no point in playing with those figures. They were hopeless.

What the pastor wanted to know was what could be done for the membership. 25 families would be facing their own mortgage payments, some on houses bigger than the church, and 12 of them would be facing funeral costs. No provision could be made for indulgence, but $5,000 per funeral already led to $60,000 in expenses.

Back to those mortgages: guesstimated average? There were massive outliers. Captain Bragg's widow had a million-dollar mortgage to deal with, for one example. One could not leave the outliers out, for those widows needed provision too, but again, there was no money for extreme indulgence. Assume $2,500 to manage those mortgages, per person, for just one month. That was another $62,500.

So: just to get through the next two weeks, the 25 families needed at least $122,500 – make it $150,000 for contingencies. *Nobody* had that kind of money to give – no group of people in the church could pull that together.

There was, however, a way the church could do it. One last way.

"They're going to kill me either way, Lord," the pastor said, "but I can't do this any way but what You tell me, and there's just this one way that only You can make happen. Guide me, Lord. I know we have a duty to care for our brothers and our sisters with our resources, to meet their needs as You meet ours without basing Your grace and mercy on our sins. I'll do whatever You tell me to do, Lord – just confirm for me that this is what You want. I'm not seeking a way out of doing this. I just want to be absolutely sure. In Jesus's precious name ... ."

"Amen."

The amen was harmonized; Rev. Willborough's light tenor had been met by a fuller, more mature one from the other side of the booth.

"Thank you, brother," the pastor said. "I can't see you, but I appreciate you joining in."

"I was not trying to eavesdrop," said the soft but full voice from the opposite side of the booth, "but it is my practice to pray with all saints I encounter who are seeking God's will earnestly, as I so often must do."

"Thank you, brother," said the pastor. "I needed that help."

"May I intercede for you, sir?"

"Please!"

"Father, in the mighty name of Jesus, I come to You first giving honor to Your holy name. May Your kingdom come and Your will be done on earth as it is in heaven, and let us be mindful of our responsibility to be the agents of Your will on this earth. Thank You for Your gracious provision of daily bread even past midnight, and we rely on You to provide for us today and tomorrow, trusting in Your promise to meet our every need.

"Father, my brother, whose face I have not yet seen, has come before You in prayer asking for clarity upon Your will, and what direction You would have him to go. Bless him, Father, with the clarity He seeks, the courage to walk the path, and protection from the enemies who would oppose You and what You want done in the situation. Help him to walk in Your Spirit, every step of the way, and to know his victory is assured by Your power.

"Also, Father, please grant my brother, and all those who know You and are seeking Your will, peace, peace in knowing You always lead us right, and will continue to lead us until we have come all the way home to You."

"We thank You for hearing all that we pray that is in Your will, and we praise You for Your endless grace and mercy upon us. We place our trust in You, and rest in Your promises. For Yours is the kingdom, and the power, and the glory, forever, Amen."

"Amen – thank You, Lord, for seating me opposite a brother in You, and I pray that you will touch him in every situation that is causing him to have to sit up on this long night, and bring him all the things He is in need of. Thank You, Lord, for Your perfect provision to all Your children, Your grace and mercy. Thank You! In Jesus' name, Amen."

Silence, except for two men so moved by this unexpected moment of earnest Christian fellowship that they were both working to control their weeping.

"Thank You, Lord – You have strengthened me, this night, to know that I am not alone in this world, in my struggle to deal with the responsibilities upon me, and to grant that I might be of help to another of Yours – thank You!" cried the fuller tenor, at last unable to control his emotions.

"Thank You, Father – yes, amen, I also am strengthened, and know now what I am to do. I have my answer, to do what You have made possible for me to do for the brothers and sisters in my care all that I can, even as this brother, in his own struggle, did all that Your Spirit moved upon him to do for me in my struggle – thank You!"

The fuller tenor did just what Rev. Willborough expected it was capable of – he burst into quiet but lovely song, on the best-known hymn of Ms. Fanny Crosby:

"Blessed assurance, Jesus is mine!
Oh, what a foretaste of glory divine!
Heir of salvation, purchase of God,

Born of His Spirit, washed in His blood!

This is my story, this is my song!

Praising my Savior, all the day long!

This is my story, this is my song!

Praising my Savior, all the day long!"

Rev. Willborough added his higher tenor to that, and a woman's voice joined in from nearby, and another man, and then another man, and another woman – five-part harmony, soft and sweet, and eventually everyone in the diner had stopped to listen to the spontaneous outpouring of joy from people who knew nothing about each other, but somehow shared the same joy, in Christ. It was brief, as no one was trying to disturb anyone else, but no one there would forget it.

Rev. Willborough heard his new friend, at the end, burst into tears – a full release, a moment of catharsis, after which there came the sound of soft snoring. Rev. Willborough carefully got up, and went to the counter.

"Here's $50," he said. "My friend has dozed off in the opposite booth, so here's for me and him, and if there's any over, I'll be back tomorrow to pay it."

The waitress at the counter smiled.

"Your new friend is a good friend," she said. "While you were praying, Harry had your bill put on his card."

"Tell Harry that Theodore thanks him," said the pastor, "and that if I'm not broke in the next four weeks, I've got the next one."

***

The week flew by for Rev. Willborough – all kinds of meetings, all stages of grief – denial, anger, depression, bargaining, acceptance – and a final, half-reluctant but settled movement toward the only way forward there was to a productive outcome.

There then remained, for Sunday, that task that only he could do: that last sermon, and the announcement that went with it. Rev. Willborough took the pulpit with his usual studied calm, and looked over his sad, sad congregation. Sorrow, and guilt, and fear were thick. Captain Hamilton, wisely, had decided to be absent with his family – nothing good could have come from him returning after that fateful Friday night that had sealed the fate of Roadside Baptist Church.

"Good morning, brothers and sisters in Christ. Please stand for the reading of the Word of God, and turn to II Chronicles 36, verses 14-16."

That caused some eyebrows to be raised – that was not a common passage of Scripture for a sermon. Little wonder.

14. Moreover all the chief of the priests, and the people, transgressed very much after all the abominations of the heathen; and polluted the house of the LORD which he had hallowed in Jerusalem.

15. And the LORD God of their fathers sent to them by his messengers, rising up betimes, and sending; because he had compassion on his people, and on his dwelling place:

16. But they mocked the messengers of God, and despised his words, and misused his prophets, until the wrath of the LORD arose against his people, till there was no remedy."

Those who knew, knew – there were few who did not understand the import of the pastor's selection.

"In context, this passage is the explanation of why the Lord allowed the kingdom of Judah, ruled over by the chosen Davidic line that would led to the Messiah, to be taken out of the Promised Land into Babylonian captivity. Despite their having the law, and the prophets, they had chosen their sins and rejected God's compassionate attempt to lead them from their evil way – until at last, there was no alternative than judgment.

"We of the church of European descent often like to think that we have displaced the Jews, and so all the promises to Israel to inherit the earth have passed to us. If that were true, then there is another corollary: if we were to behave as the heathen behave, then the promise of God's judgment would also belong to us. We never think of that part, but because God ever is intolerant of sin, His judgment of it is ever inevitable.

"Yet I do not speak of some future date of God completing the present age, or even of Israel's sad past. I speak of only two weeks ago, Friday, in which day, this church, after three years of teaching of the Gospel, and the duties incumbent upon its believers in terms of how they are to treat brethren and neighbors in light of all racial and cultural divisions being subordinated to Christian unity and duty to the dying world, chose to become a rallying point for domestic terrorism, in a complete and final rejection of God's will.

"For ancient Judah, the Chaldeans arrive in verse 17. Two weeks ago Friday, 25 men of this church were given into the hands of Captain Ironwood Hamilton and the law enforcement agents and community members with him who made their stand at the Gilligan House. They want not a man of their number; they have no serious injuries.

"Yet we are mortally wounded. Without those 25 men, Roadside is at this moment insolvent. We cannot pay our bills to the end of the month, and certainly the mortgage is unattainable. More importantly; we have no resources to help the 25 families facing funeral costs and mortgage payments. *There is no remedy,* church. Roadside is finished, and, economically, so are many of you."

That settled like the pall of death over the whole assembly.

"If God did not spare ancient Judah, why did we assume He would spare us, when He does not change? Is it because for so long, we were able to put other families in the situations we now are in, in order to live a lifestyle we have not earned and did not deserve? Is it because over our long years of such sin, we became more and more deaf to God's voice warning us? Do we yet hear now?

"Yet, know this: the grim chapter which I have spoken of ends with hope, for the sin of Judah did not end the purposes of God with the nation, and after 70 years, God raised King Cyrus to the throne of Persia in order that the Jews might return home, and there be as the time of the Messiah drew near and at last dawned from Israel upon the world. As ever, God tempered His judgment with mercy, a mercy rooted in His plan to redeem mankind to Himself.

"This mercy of God, and His love, is best expressed in John 3:16 – for God so loved the world that He gave Himself, in the person of His only begotten son, the Lord Jesus Christ, that whosoever believeth in Him should not perish – not be forever condemned in their sin – but have everlasting life. That it is to the world should tell us of God's regard for every family, tribe, and nation – each and every one was worth the shedding of His precious blood – and should tell everyone in this room that salvation, or forgiveness for the saved in sin, is available to all. Even you. Even me.

"For us: the wideness of that mercy provides that there is an investor who desires to purchase this building, for enough to pay off the bills, the mortgage, and provide around $175,000 left. This will be enough for us to make a grant to the Lofton County Emergency Fund, in the name of this church, to provide those of you who sign up for that grant to get help with your funeral expenses and your mortgage for the next month. After that, Roadside will have disposed of its assets, and will close down, orderly. Today is the last day, therefore, of services."

By this point, the silence had been broken by many people, weeping

– many, many people. Many people sat with angry faces, others were just shocked. Rev. Willborough could not restrain his own tears.

"What benediction, what final words of blessing, shall I say over you, in this my last sermon, and the last in which we shall be together? I offer you the only comfort that will do you good. The wideness of God's mercy still is available in forgiveness for all. The work of Christ, in that He died on the cross for the sins of the world, was buried, and rose again on the third day, is effective and available to every one of us.

"It is necessary, however, to agree with God about our sin, and come to Him with no thought of dragging our favorite sins behind us. Do not bother to insult God and waste your time if you seek a salvation or restoration of good standing with Him if you intend to cling to the prideful, malicious, wicked *racist* ways that have brought us all to this terrible end."

Rev. Willborough took a deep breath, and put forth all his courage.

"Instead, go directly to *the devil,* racist Christian, that he might sift you as wheat and inadvertently arrange for God to add whatever chastening is necessary to get you ready to confess and repent and return to Him. Racist unbeliever – savage, unwashed heathen – if you will not turn, then go *the devil* and declare your allegiance to the devilry that you love, and cease to trouble the church of God."

"To the rest: come to God, in repentance and faith, and He will receive you, as sons and daughters new and old. With that, I leave you. You are dismissed. Anyone who wishes to speak with me about the path to salvation, or restoration, I will be at the Tinyville Diner for the rest of the afternoon."

Rev. Willborough closed his Bible, sat down, and watched his congregation, looking stunned and drained, file out for the last time. There was no postlude: the musician was in the Tinyville jail, and the church certainly could not afford to hire another one.

When the building was empty but for the trustees and deacons, they and the pastor went out, and the locksmith they had hired stepped out of his truck, was paid out of the deacons, trustees, and pastor's pockets, and then changed all the locks. Then, it was done. The organized church history of a combined 180 years thus ended.

Epilogue 3: Further Vignettes from the Flames

"Folks just do not learn," said Ms. Maggie Thornton, secretary to the police commissioner's office in Big Loft, VA.

Ms. Thornton's heart was aching, as she was watching her fifth commissioner in five months be appointed. The last one had only lasted five days.

All four there before Acting Commissioner Tate had made the same mistake.

They had attempted to manipulate the man she loved.

Captain Henry Fitzhugh Lee was tall, well-built, and very handsome, being in appearance very like the Lee relative whom Virginia had made an idol of. He also had the same general habits; quiet, humble, brilliant, and, if not bothered, perfectly mild-mannered. He had been brought in to work cold cases, and quietly went about solving one every ten days if left alone.

But, Commissioner Thomas had added to the captain's assignment: a big, dangerous Freedom of Information Act project. The commissioner had then attempted to manipulate Captain Lee into producing results favorable to the department. That had tipped Captain Lee off to the commissioner's corruption, and within five days, Commissioner Thomas had died resisting arrest, with two of his three deputies jailed to await trial.

The third deputy, made acting commissioner, had died from the stress of trying to intimidate Captain Lee.

Right. The man trying to intimidate Captain Lee had died of the stress of trying to do that.

And now here was Acting Commissioner Tate, going through Captain Lee's file talking about, "there's got to be some way to break him down a little."

Ms. Thornton just knew that office was going to see a sixth commissioner before it was done. There were just some men you didn't need to bother to manipulate.

Ms. Thornton saw Captain Lee in passing later that afternoon, walking with one of the lieutenants assigned to work with him on his cases. She had just stood still for a moment, and watched, happily dazzled, as the captain had paused in his conversation long enough to smile and acknowledge her presence with a sweet smile and a greeting. He should have been on administrative leave, but nobody had gotten around to putting him on it.

So, Captain Lee rolled right on, and Ms. Thornton was glad.

"Maybe," she said to herself, "those that just won't learn and change will get cleaned out of here, rubbing up against our good Harry," she said. "I don't know why they just didn't make straightforward Chief Scott commissioner anyway, but the way things are going, he will be in the office soon, and then maybe things will get right."

***

"A smile opens a lot of doors, Harry," said Horace Fitzhugh Lee one fine day in 1980 to his overly serious little grandson Henry, "and if you take please, thank you, and a firm handshake with you through those doors, you can go just about anywhere you want."

"But what if I don't feel like smiling?" said little Henry.

"We're not talking about how you feel," said Grandpa, gently. "I'm telling you how you get where you want to go in life. If you can get where you want to go, you'll feel better about life."

In mature manhood, Henry Fitzhugh Lee blessed God for his grandfather's teaching every day, but especially since coming to his third career: police captain in the half-destroyed police force of Big Loft, VA. Especially since he had done half of the destroying, and not quite inadvertently.

Captain Lee had a striking resemblance to his Southern-idol great-great-great-uncle General R.E. Lee, and in Virginia that opened all kinds of doors all by itself, but that wasn't what had allowed him to survive.

It was the smile, the smile and thank you for those downhearted and discouraged in the police department's Human Resources offices, who had been willing to tell him what to look out for even before he had done his interview with the department big wigs.

It was the smile and the please and the thank you for all the secretaries and janitors and junior officers, all of whom were being treated barely above slaves by the corrupt big wigs that infested headquarters, some of whom who just were looking for a reason to leave … or to stay, and fight for the right, but just needed some support, somewhere.

It was the smile and the handshake and the calm, reasoned, and well-considered orders that had told many captains and lieutenants who knew about the corruption in the commissioner's office and were about to go prematurely bald because they needed their jobs and couldn't afford to be whistleblowers – it was the smile that had told them that there was at last a man with power in the situation who was stoutly for the right, and they should just hang on a little longer … .

Or at least, that was how all those smiles had been interpreted. People made of them what they wanted, as they made of their friendships … but what it let them know about Captain Lee was that he was not an enemy to the right, but a friend.

Now, those who had survived had a whole police department to put back together.

Captain Lee came to work every day, in unspeakable pain over what he had needed to do to give the honest people in that department that chance. That had not been a smiling matter.

Yet he kept smiling at his fellow survivors, and the people who were for the right kept going through all the open doors now existing in the future of Big Loft's police force.

Ms. Thornton from the commissioner's office always seemed especially in need of a smile … five commissioners in five months, and this noble, honest woman stayed and worked without complaint … Captain Lee always put a little extra on his smile for her, and she seemed to glow and stay encouraged.

***

When you are a bigwig in a corrupt hierarchy, you just can never tell when and how judgment may come, even if you have escaped public exposure and punishment for your deeds while others did not.

You might have the Angel of Death two floors below you, still on the payroll, for example.

Acting Commissioner Tate of the police force of Big Loft, VA did not believe until about one second before he died.

He had it all worked out, how he was going to make that utterly deathly creature known to his rational mind as Captain H.F. Lee become fully mortal and disappear forever.

Three men above the third-day-in-office-commissioner – Commissioner Thomas and his two favorite deputies – had disappeared after their corruption had been exposed. Captain Lee had arrested the deputies and outright killed the commissioner when he resisted arrest by shooting first.

The first acting commissioner had gotten so stressed in trying to intimidate said captain that he had a heart attack while trying to do it and died.

But, Acting Commissioner Tate knew he had a foolproof plan, and, after three days of planning it, began the walk down the front staircase at police headquarters, two flights down to the second floor, on which, at the end of a nondescript little hallway, Captain Lee was doubtless in his lonely office, still not placed on leave, still working his cold cases … .

The acting commissioner went down that front staircase, whose huge plate glass windows made up the centerpiece of the building façade that made the headquarters the envy of all other departments in Lofton County … .

That front staircase, that had such fine acoustics …

Acting Commissioner Tate was rehearsing his speech as he approached the second floor landing, feeling himself prepared to confront the fully mortal captain, and had just mentioned the captain's name as forcefully as his imagination would allow.

But as it is said, speak of the devil, and he appears … the Angel of Death was no exception, because he was coming down from the third floor after consulting some records for a cold case he was working. Thus, the instant the commissioner spoke his name, the commissioner heard the creature's step behind him, and heard that calm, terrible voice floating angelically down...

"Good morning, Commissioner – I am here."

Acting Commissioner Tate really didn't want to see Captain Lee after all, so much so that he jumped from the sheer terror he had been trying to deny he felt, missed the last step before the landing, careened helplessly forward, crashed into and through the plate glass window, and fell two floors to the sidewalk and his death.

***

"It's a fake video – it's CLEARLY a fake video – can't you get this cleaned up in time for the press conference?"

This was the mayor of Big Loft, VA, he and his office already reeling from the death of the fifth police commissioner in as many weeks. But also, someone had dropped a video to his office purporting to show three of those men involved in deep financial corruption – making deals to arrest and convict so many Black people in the city per year to fill up neighboring Roanoke County's new private prison.

The problem was, the video was clearly a fake – several other figures were just the three commissioners, layered over other figures with different voices added. The marvels of CGI...

The mayor wanted it fixed by the press conference, and it was, halfway through, as the mayor blasted all of the press, both the mainstream and the Lofton County Free Voice, the new confrontational

Black newspaper, for seizing on and blowing up fake news.

Halfway through, the cleaned-up video arrived, in the hands of a very pale-looking aide.

"Sir, it's fixed, but I don't think you want to –."

The mayor didn't even hear that; he snatched the video from the aide who brought it, and handed it to the one running the video and big screen in the chamber where the press conference was being held.

"All right, you tabloid pushers – now, you're going to see what is REALLY going on! I expect your retractions QUICK!"

The cleaned-up video showed crystal-clear, with no duplicate figures … instead, the other figures beside the late Commissioner Thomas and his two favorite deputies turned out to be the vice mayor, the president of the county board of supervisors, the county prosecutor, and several police officers from Lofton County's smaller towns, talking false arrests, big money, and what they were going to buy with all of that.

Silence reigned for a few moments, and then all the papers got photos of the mayor's open mouth, and quoted him as he cried out before falling out, outright –.

"Go back to the fake video! Go back to the fake video! Somebody, anybody – go back to the fake one! Oh, NOOOOOOOOOOOOOOOOOOOOOOOOOOOOOOOOOOOOOOOO!"

***

Spent and tired – if there were three words to describe many people in Lofton County, VA on the third weekend after the Gilligan House Burning, those were it.

61 percent of the county was tired of seeing themselves represented in the news as rank, relentless, heartless, but ultimately helpless criminals, collapsing under the weight of their own evil. Five police commissioners in a row, the mayor and the vice mayor of Big Loft, the county's biggest city, had fallen; half the county board of supervisors, the county prosecutors, and members or former members of every police department in the county were exposed.

The news was so bad that the Black and Latino citizens of Lofton County, who usually were portrayed as the only bad guys in the world, could not even get their usual airtime – the crimes of poverty were too petty by comparison to the crimes of affluence and power being revealed among the superiors of those who thought themselves superior.

Meanwhile, over root beer floats, James Varick IV, Harvey

Harrison, and Thomas Stepforth Sr. were also spent and tired, but smiling. These three principals of the *Lofton County Free Voice,* the first Black newspaper to survive in Lofton County *ever,* remembered the first day that they posted up the first issue of the paper, called the wickedness now exposed what it was, demanded the data that proved it, and walked by faith … to a first victory.

"Mission #1 accomplished," said Mr. Stepforth.

"Right," said Mr. Varick. "We're not going to let up; now it is time to use our leverage to get organs of power in this county and its towns the way we need them to be for our descendants."

"Right," said Mr. Harrison. "While exposure runs its course, we implement Phase 2."

Mr. Varick chuckled.

"They can't handle Phase 1, and it's not done. They sho' 'nuff ain't gonna be ready for Phase 2, and then Phase 3 … but they will have to learn!"